THE INCREDIBLE BILLY WILD

Also by Joanna Nadin

Joe All Alone

White Lies, Black Dare

THE INCREDIBLE BILLY WILD

JOANNA NADIN

LITTLE, BROWN BOOKS FOR YOUNG READERS
www.lbkids.co.uk

LITTLE, BROWN BOOKS FOR YOUNG READERS

First published in Great Britain in 2017 by Hodder and Stoughton

1 3 5 7 9 10 8 6 4 2

All characters and events in this publication, other than those clearly in the public domain, are fictitious and any resemblance to real persons, living or dead, is purely coincidental.

A CIP catalogue record for this book
is available from the British Library.

ISBN 978-1-51020-125-5

Printed and bound by CPI Group (UK) Ltd, Croydon, CR0 4YY

The paper and board used in this book are
made from wood from responsible sources.

Little, Brown Books for Young Readers
An imprint of
Hachette Children's Group
Part of Hodder and Stoughton
Carmelite House
50 Victoria Embankment
London EC4Y 0DZ

An Hachette UK Company
www.hachette.co.uk

www.hachettechildrens.co.uk

For Karen Ball,

who said "write about a dog"

Dear Dog,

It was Mum who gave me the name.

"You're incredible," she'd say as she swung me up into the air. "Do you know that? The Incredible Billy Wild."

I don't remember that much about her – I was only four then – but that stuck. Or maybe I just held on to it harder than all the other stuff. Whichever, the older I got, the less I understood why she'd even said it at all, because I wasn't that incredible at anything. I'm fourth slowest at running in our class including the girls. I can't juggle or do somersaults or even keep a football in the air for more than a single kick. And, like Miss Merriott says, my spelling isn't all it could be.

So I started to think maybe I'd imagined it, or maybe The Incredible Billy Wild was another boy entirely. Not me, after all.

That's what I thought, until I found you.

Imagine if I hadn't.

Imagine if I'd not gone to the shed that day. Or imagine if I'd called the police. Or, worst of all, imagine if I'd taken you back like I was supposed to.

I wouldn't be The Incredible Billy Wild. And you wouldn't have a name at all. You'd be just another Good-For-Nowt waiting for the bolt.

Imagine that, Dog.

Sunday March 13th
5.30 p.m.

Dear God,

It was my teacher Miss Merriott's idea. She said for holiday homework we had to write to you.

Seamus Patterson said he didn't believe in God, not the bloke with the white beard in the sky anyway, because that was mental. And Hassan Farooq said he believed in Allah so he couldn't do it either. But Miss Merriott said Allah *was* a god, and all religions had a god, just different versions, and we could make up our own gods if we didn't have one. The point was to write to them to tell them what we'd done every day, and what we'd like to change in the world, like a sort of prayer and a diary all in one. We could say anything at all because it was private and only she and maybe the god we'd written to would see.

When she said that, everyone went bonkers making up gods with laser eyes and flame-throwing fingers and the power to turn Mrs Johnson the dinner lady into a bat. Except for me. I was too busy thinking of what I wanted, which is:

- A dog. Preferably a Great Dane, because I could probably ride that, or a dachshund because it would fit in my book bag. But if not any old dog will do.
- For Seamus Patterson to disappear. Or maybe even turn into a dog. Although knowing my luck he'd be a mean one that was mainly teeth.
- To be incredible.

The Seamus Patterson bit is because he once stuck a plastic soldier up my nose and still calls me Billy Weird and then does a laughing sound.

The incredible bit is because it's the Brimley's Got Talent show on Easter Monday, which is two weeks today, and loads of my class are going to do it. Manjit Patel's doing keepy-uppy, Julie Gilhoolie's playing recorder and Paris Potts is going to sing "Price Tag" by Jessie J. At home time Miss Merriott asked if I was entering and I thought of my mum then. She used to call me The Incredible Billy Wild, like I was full of talent. Only I don't know what that talent is, and she's dead now so I can't ask her. My brother Tommo, he's the brainy one, even though he's only six. And Johnny's fourteen and annoying, but he also knows all the lines from all the *Star Wars* films and is dead good at skateboarding.

But me? I'm just Billy. So if you could make me a bit incredible at something, that would be immense.

Anyway, I hope all this is OK, talking to you like this. It feels a bit weird if I'm honest, but not totally horrible. Though if Johnny found out he'd probably say I was a little knob. He calls me that a lot, *and* he smokes cigarettes. Other Nan says Johnny's going Off The Rails.

Do you know Johnny? You probably do because you can see all of us – at least that's what we learned in the Sunday school that Other Nan made us go to after Mum died. But in case you don't, he is tallish and thinnish and mainly frowns. His hair is sort of plain brown and not in any style at all, except too long, according to Other Nan, who has told him to get it cut a bazillion times. Tommo has almost no hair because he got nits so Dad shaved it because it was cheaper than the shampoo.

Tommo's mainly into *Star Wars* and swaps. Yesterday he swapped his bobble hat for two mini Mars bars. Dad's going to go bonkers when he finds out, only he can't make Tommo swap them back, like he did with the door keys and the Transformers sticker, because Tommo's eaten them already.

Dad's going bonkers a lot these days. He was cross with me yesterday afternoon for leaving my bike out, and then he was cross when I did put it away because I slammed the shed door and he says it's going to break soon if I keep doing that. I said the shed's mostly broken anyway but he said, "I'm not blind, Billy. I'll fix it as soon as I get some time when I'm not working or dealing with You Boys which probably won't be until Kingdom Come." I asked when Kingdom might Come and he said not for at least two weeks because he's working extra shifts at the hospital because of the strike.

He's a midwife, which is a person who helps ladies have babies. They look inside them to see if it's time for the baby to come out, and then they say "you're doing well, keep pushing" and things like that. Most people, for instance Other Nan and Seamus Patterson, think it's a weird job for a man but me and Tommo think it's dead interesting. Tommo is especially interested in things to do with women. He says it's because the house is so full of testosterone, which is a hormone for boys only and makes us smell and get angry. Women have *eestro*-something which does other stuff to do with eggs, which we learned in school, only I'm not too sure about it all because Seamus Patterson was saying "ugggh" loudly in that bit.

Anyway, the midwives and a lot of other nurses are going on strike soon because they're not being paid enough. Only when they go on strike they won't get paid at all, which Dad said is Sod's Law. So he's working all he can now to make up for it, which means Mum's friend Aunty Geena comes to babysit a lot. I like Geena because she's into Lego and lets me draw on her iPad. Johnny hates it when she comes because he says he's not a baby and Tommo mainly sighs because he says even though Aunty Geena is a woman, she is not very good at cleaning or cooking, which means she does not have the Woman's Touch. Tommo is desperate for our house to have the Woman's Touch because, as he says, how many normal people have to microwave their pants dry because their dad has forgotten to hang the washing out? Dad said we could wear his but we said we'd rather not, thank you.

Tommo got the Woman's Touch thing off Other Nan, who is Mum's mum. But she's only saying it because she doesn't want Us Boys to live with Dad any more. She thinks we should move in with her on the other side of town because she's retired and has nothing to do except Charitable Deeds. Dad says no one is moving anywhere unless it's over his dead body. I don't suppose Other Nan would mind that as she is not madly keen on Dad. She's not keen on a lot of things, for instance fizzy drinks, shaved bits in hairdos and orange tans, but it is mainly Dad who is the problem.

Me and Tommo worked out all the things she doesn't like about him and the top five are:

- He is a midwife, which is woman's work, and also weird because he is only doing it because Mum died and it won't bring her back.
- He wears trainers instead of actual shoes.
- He likes football not rugby.
- His mum, Nice Nan, has an orange face.
- His favourite TV programmes are football; *Storage Wars*, which is where people buy other people's storage cupboards in case there is treasure in them only there usually isn't; *Wheeler Dealers*, which is mostly sweaty men fixing cars; and *The One Show*, because it has a bit of everything.

Other Nan only likes the news, *Songs of Praise*, which is mostly old people all singing about you, and things with David Attenborough in them. She says we're being deprived of a proper childhood because of the bad telly and Dad being at work a lot, which is also why Johnny is going Off The Rails. This is because her neighbour Mr Norris saw Johnny sitting in the bus shelter with Fergal Patterson, who is Seamus's big brother. They were kicking an empty Fanta bottle and it hit Mr Norris's dog but Johnny didn't say anything not even sorry and Fergal said a really bad swear. So Mr Norris told Other Nan who told Dad who asked Johnny about it.

Johnny said, "I didn't say the f word, so why is it my fault?"

Dad said, "But you didn't stop him saying the f word, or tell him he shouldn't."

And Johnny said, "*You* try telling Fergal not to say the f word. If you want a smack."

Tommo said, "I know the f word." But everyone ignored him.

Dad said, "I don't know why you hang around with that boy in the first place."

Johnny didn't have anything to say to that so he just stormed off to his room and slammed the door, which Tommo said was a definite sign of being Off The Rails.

Anyway, Other Nan's wrong about Dad depriving us of our childhood, because he's let me and Tommo put the pop-up tent up in our bedroom so we can camp tonight. We wanted to put it in the garden but Dad says it's too cold and wet plus it'll only get nicked.

It's not a massive tent, God, in case you were imagining the ones like in the desert or something. It's for two people and it folds down into a circle that is about the size of, say, a sink. Only when it's popped it takes up more space than you would think, because there's not much room to walk around our room now. Plus it springed so hard that it pinged Dad in the face and knocked Tommo's Transformers off the windowsill. Tommo started crying because they're all out of order now and he'll have to arrange them again. But he stopped once Dad told us to get inside and make our beds.

Mine's like a nest. It's got my sleeping bag and a cushion for a pillow, and under the pillow I've got my precious things, which are:

- A cat's eye. Not a real one, one of the ones that glow on the road at night, and which is just a glass marble, really.
- A torch so we can see, and also do Morse Code.
- A ball made completely of elastic bands.
- Mum's second best ring, which had a red stone in it called a garnet, only the stone fell out and got lost so Dad glued in a tiny pasta shell which I felt-tipped red.

It's dead good in here, God. All orange and cosy and glowing. It feels small but safe. Tommo curled up and said it was like being inside a womb, only without all the blood and stuff. Dad said there was no way he could remember that but Tommo said "can too" and Dad didn't argue even though we all know Tommo's lying. And I wished I could remember being inside Mum, but then I thought, *At least I can remember Tommo being in there*, which I told him, which made him happy. Then Dad went downstairs and we both lay in here for a bit all snuggled sideways, and then Tommo left to have a wee and watch telly so he's gone now. But it still feels warm and womb-like and I feel calm.

Maybe it's because I get to sleep in a tent even if it is inside the house. Or maybe it's because it's the holidays so I won't see Seamus Patterson for two whole weeks. Or maybe it's just that I'm enjoying telling you stuff because now I've said all the thoughts, they don't seem to be swirling round in my head so much.

I have to stop now, though, because Dad just shouted up to say tea's ready, and if I'm late Johnny will steal my Alphabites, which in case you don't know are potatoes shaped like letters of the alphabet and are delicious.

Bye then, God.

PS I just thought of something else. If you've got time, I'd also like some new Nerf darts, and an iPhone and also world peace, because I heard

Paris Potts say she was going to put that and my other things are just for me, which is a bit selfish. Thanks!

8.30 p.m.

It's much later now and Tommo is asleep but I'm not, I'm in the bathroom, pretending to have a wee but actually talking to you, which is sort of a lie only no one has noticed so I don't think it counts.

After tea, Dad said if it's not raining tomorrow we can have a campfire instead of normal lunch because he's off shift, and then maybe we can go up the garden centre to look for a new shed. Only then Tommo said chance would be a fine thing, because Dad is always promising stuff like that and it doesn't often happen. So then Dad stamped out of the kitchen and slammed the door and Johnny called Tommo a bad word, because now Dad won't give Johnny a fiver to go out later.

But the thing is, God, I have faith, which is

when you believe in something even when you know it might not happen or even be real.

A bit like believing in you, I suppose.

Bye again.

PS I'm not sure if it's OK just to say "bye" but "amen" is for the god in church and in my head you're more like Mr Nesbit, who is our headmaster. Only you have better hair and you don't smell of soup.

Monday March 14th

11 a.m.

Dear God,

Tommo was right after all. Big Sue called, who is the boss of Dad's ward, and asked Dad to go back into work. He said yes because of needing the money for a new shed, and because of the strike, and also Tommo has grown out of his school shoes again. But then he called up Aunty Geena on speaker while he did the washing-up and it turns out she's gone to Kettering because her mum's got shingles.

Dad said, "Bloody hell, Geena, when were you going to tell me? You were supposed to be sitting tomorrow as it is."

She said, "Sorry, Danny. It's been hell on legs here. I forgot."

Dad said, "Christ on a bike. *Now* what am I going to do?"

Geena said, "What about your mother-in-law?"

And me and Tommo gasped at that, because Dad's mother-in-law is Other Nan, and even Dad says it's like having a Dalek as a nanny when she babysits. Then we did a sigh of relief because Dad said, "I'd rather stick needles in my eyes."

Geena said, "Fair point. Can't Johnny manage?"

And I said, "No!"

And Tommo said, "No!"

But Dad said, "Beggars can't be choosers, I suppose."

So now Johnny's in charge. Which I'm not too pleased about because it means no campfire. Johnny's not too pleased because of us being

Annoying Little Knobs, but Dad's sorted it so Tommo's going round Sonny Potts's house so it's only me to look after. And he's left out ham for sandwiches and a tenner for fish and chips for tea. Plus he'll let Johnny off the pound for the swear jar for saying knob. Johnny didn't have time to think of an answer because then Dad's friend Karol, who's actually a man, which Tommo thinks is even funnier than the boy on YouTube who can burp *Chopsticks*, was honking his silver Nissan Micra outside, so Dad had to go or he'd miss his lift.

So now I'm stuck at home on the first day of the holidays with no campfire, no shed-buying trip and not even Tommo. Johnny doesn't want to play Lego or any of the other ideas I suggested. He doesn't even want to talk to me. At the moment he's in his room playing music about death loudly, but what if he decides to go Off The Rails today, like Other Nan says? Or what if aliens decide this morning is a good time to land and take over Earth and they choose our back garden and it's only me and Johnny to defend the planet? Although so far the most interesting things to happen in our part of town are:

- When Mr Lomax found an unexploded bomb in his back garden and the army closed down the road, only it turned out to be an old petrol can.
- When Philip Ratchet who is in the year above Johnny tried to rob Mrs Beasley at the corner shop, only she recognised his balaclava because she'd knitted it and she called his mum and he was in massive trouble for months.
- When Nice Nan won a thousand pounds on the bingo and moved to Spain with Maurice Watson off the Internet. Mrs Beasley said it was inappropriate and Other Nan said it was typical but we thought it was OK because she gave us twenty pounds

each and we're going to stay in Malaga in
the summer.

But that was a year ago and nothing exciting has happened since. So it's unlikely that anything will happen today, especially not aliens because they're not real. Tommo says they are but that's only because of *Star Wars* and anyway I Googled it and there's no scientific proof.

So I'm just staying in the tent for now. And if I get bored then I've got you to talk to, God. The more I do it, the more I like talking to you. I might even carry on after this homework's done – after Easter, I mean. If that's all right with you. Miss Merriott's always saying it helps to talk, for instance when I get picked last in PE, or if Seamus Patterson's called me a spanner, or when it's Mother's Day. And I know Miss Merriott means talk to her, or Dad, or even Johnny. But if I do talk to her Seamus Patterson might hear, and I can't talk to Dad because he's too busy, or

Johnny because he'll just call me a knob, so that leaves you.

Bye for now.

4 p.m.

Dear God,

Something happened. Which maybe you already know. But in case not, what actually happened is this:

At about half-eleven, Johnny came in and said he'd got a text from Leia (who is his girlfriend and is half from Poland and also a goth). She wanted to meet him down the skate park so I had to go too, but could I not hang around him the whole time and make him look like a knob. I said fine but could I have a snack first, for instance some cheese on Digestives, which sounds weird but is actually an excellent combination, only Johnny said there wasn't time and he'd get me a Mars on the way. I thought that sounded fair so I got my coat and went to the shed to fetch my bike, which is when it all started. Because when I got there the door wasn't shut.

I felt sick then, like when you go over a humpback bridge too fast. I knew Johnny hadn't left it open because he keeps his skateboard under his bed with his magazines and cigarettes and other secret stuff. So I knew it must be my fault for slamming the shed door, which had broken after all, and probably my bike had been burgled and the old lawnmower too and that meant I was in Big Trouble. Bigger even than the time me and Tommo left the tap running upstairs when we were playing submarines, only Dad called us down for tea and water came through the ceiling into the fish fingers. Which Tommo said was more realistic for the fish but Dad didn't agree.

Anyway, when I went in the shed, the bike was still there and the lawnmower and the old bin bags of baby clothes that Dad hadn't yet taken down the charity shop. I did an actual noise out loud like I'd been holding my breath and hadn't even known it, because I was so happy. But then I sucked the breath back in because I saw that the bags were all ripped and the clothes were scattered around and some of them looked like they'd been chewed. And I could see exactly who had chewed them. And I knew then that you'd listened to me. You'd REALLY listened!

Because curled up on the floor, asleep in a nest of old babygrows, with a hat made out of a dinosaur T-shirt and a box of empty bird seed still in its mouth, was a real, live dog.

It wasn't a Great Dane, or even a dachshund. It was a greyhound, which I know because Nice Nan, the one who's in Spain with Maurice off the Internet, used to take us to the dog-racing sometimes. Only this one didn't look so much like those dogs, all shiny and sleek. This one was thin and pale and shivery, and it smelled of old wee like Dead Grandpa used to. If I hadn't seen its thin ribs go up and down with its breaths, I'd have maybe thought it was a ghost of a greyhound come to haunt us. I was just thinking how amazing a ghost greyhound would be, only not more amazing than a real one, when Johnny shouted, "Come on, Billy! Shift it!"

I had to think really quickly then and the thought I came up with was to shut the door and go back into the house saying "I feel sick". Which I know is a lie but I think it's one of those lies that are for a good cause. Like when Mum used to say "does my bum look big in this?" and Dad would give me a "zip it" look which means be quiet and then he'd say "no way", only her bum did look big.

Johnny said, "Are you serious?" I nodded and clutched my tummy a bit for effect. But then I thought that might make Johnny stay behind or call Dad, and I didn't want either of those things to happen, so I unclutched it and said I probably just needed to eat something or have a poo, which is what Dad says ninety-nine per cent of stomach aches are. Johnny said I should have gone earlier and he was going to be late now. But I said why didn't he go by himself and if I was actually sick I'd text him so he could get home before Dad. Johnny said OK, but to definitely text him if there was an emergency, and then he was gone. And then it was just me and the shed with the dog in it.

I don't know if you have the same feelings as people, God, or even if other people have the same feelings as me, but it was like the air in the kitchen was crackling with a sort of electricity. And the electricity was called possibility. Because right then I knew that anything could happen.

I waited for the front door to slam, then I ran back to the shed and opened the door gently so as not to wake the dog. But I think the yelling from before must have woken it because it wasn't on the nest any more. It was in the dark bit behind the lawnmower and its legs were trembling. It looked like it had seen a ghost, only this time the ghost was me. I said, "It's OK, it's Billy." But the dog didn't seem to think that was any better than a ghost because it squished itself even further into the dark. Then I had an idea. I said "wait here" and ran to the fridge to get the ham for lunch.

There were six slices and I took them all, because Johnny says he's being vegetarian because Leia said all meat is murder, even Peperami, and I don't mind just having cheese instead. Then I took them back to the shed and held one out to the dog, but it still didn't want to move. So I crouched down and shuffled on my knees across the floor towards the dog until I was really near and could hear its breathing, which was really fast now, and I held out the ham. This time it snapped it up and nearly snapped my hand too and I panicked and pulled it back. But then I thought maybe the dog was more scared than me, so I said "well done" and, even though my hand was shaky, I held out another piece of ham, only I shuffled back a bit so the dog had to move to get the meat, and it did. And then it moved again until it was right out in the garden with its legs still trembling but with my hand stroking its neck and six bits of ham in its belly.

Only then I'd run out of plans. The dog didn't have a collar on so there was no name and no number to call, like you're supposed to. Probably what I should have done is just ring the police or the RSPCA or even Mr Collins from Number 42 who has two Shar-Peis called Alf and Rita and knows what to do with dogs.

But I didn't.

Instead I got a babygrow out of one of the bin bags and put it round its neck as a sort of lead and by using that and waggling my hammy fingers I got the dog up the garden path and into the house.

And that's where we are now, God. Still in the house. Or actually, if you want to be factual about it, I'm on my bed and the dog is in the tent. It wanted to go into the downstairs toilet first. And then the larder. I worked out that it liked small spaces, so I showed it the tent and it went straight in and laid down. And in a minute I'm going to lie down with it. And then when Dad comes home maybe I'll say he can take down the tent now and he'll see the dog inside and his heart will melt and it will be like in a film and the dog will bring everyone together, including Other Nan, even though Dad says her heart's made of flaming stone, which is not actually meltable.

Until then, Johnny is out, and Tommo is with his friend, but I've got someone to play with. I know it's not a person, just a dog, and it can't do Minecraft or Lego or even talk back. But it's still nice to have it around. It's company, which is what Nice Nan says is the best thing about Maurice. That and his ability to win on the horses.

8 p.m.

Dear God,

Something else mad happened.

I was sitting in the tent just looking at the dog thinking it was sort of like a dragon, with its long face, only a delicate one, when the doorbell went. I had a panic then because what if it was Other Nan, or the police doing random checks for children being at home on their own, which isn't illegal but is inadvisable, according to Tommo who Googled it. And then Dad would be in trouble for doing something inadvisable. But then I thought what if it was someone important, or just Johnny who'd forgotten his keys so I answered it. Only it wasn't the police or Other Nan, or Johnny or someone important, it was Paris Potts with Sonny and Tommo, who had faces painted like a tiger and a butterfly.

She said, "Why didn't your Johnny come to collect Tommo like he was supposed to?"

I could feel my face going red then, because I don't talk to the girls in my class. I don't really talk to anyone. But Paris had her hands on her hips and her eyebrows all up in the air like she was waiting for an answer, so I said, "Something came up." Which isn't even a lie.

But she said, "A likely story."

So I decided to change the subject and asked her why was Tommo a butterfly. She said because he chose it and she couldn't do Chewbacca which was his first choice. Then, and this is the mad bit, God, she walked right into our living room with Tommo and Sonny following after her. Paris Potts from school was in my house! That's the first time anyone from school's been round mine, unless you count when Manjit Patel knocked on our door by mistake because he thought Harvey Monks lived here. Anyway, Tommo was getting upset then because of us being home alone, which was inadvisable, and said he was going to call Dad. But I told him not to because Johnny would be back any minute.

Tommo said, "What if he's not? What if he's gone Off The Rails and is in prison or has run away to America?" Tommo is very keen on America, and on all of us running away there, because of the wide choice of burger varieties. "Then we'll be alone for hours and the police will come," he carried on.

I said, "He hasn't run away. And anyway, we're not alone."

Tommo said, "Yes we are."

And I said, "No we're not."

And he said, "Yes we are."

And Paris said, "Yes you are, Billy Wild, you're all on your own, so stop telling fat ones."

And then I was feeling all hot and twitchy, partly because of Paris being here, and partly like I had this jumping bean inside me or a nugget of fire, and the nugget was the dog and it wanted to come out so I shouted, "No we're not, because God's sent someone to watch over us so the police won't mind."

Tommo's eyes went really wide then, like he'd seen a ghost, or a man swallow a sword like we saw at the circus once. He said, "Is it Nice Nan and Maurice?"

When I said no, he and Paris and Sonny did guessing, for instance Dr Who and Han Solo and everyone off *Coronation Street*. But I said it wasn't any of them and if I showed them they had to promise to be calm and especially not to shriek, which Sonny does a lot, especially when he's had a lot of Haribo which is most of the time. Paris said it had better be something good after all this dramatic build-up.

I led them upstairs into the bedroom, all tiptoeing and shushing, and then I lifted up the flap of the tent and said "Ta-dah!" Which is when Sonny did a massive shriek, and the dog did a howl and ran out of the tent and down the stairs. The next thing we know there's a massive crash in the living room and then a sound like when Tommo dropped Other Nan's china shepherdess on the patio. Paris said "Omigod" and Tommo said "Uh-oh" and I felt that humpback bridge feeling again.

When we got down to the living room the feeling didn't go away. It turned out the dog had knocked into the sideboard and the photo of Mum and Us Boys on the seesaw in Scarborough had fallen on to the floor and the glass had smashed. Tommo started crying.

Paris said, "He's probably cut himself. He might bleed out. We'll have to call nine nine nine!" She made Tommo hold out his hands but there was no blood.

Then I knew why he was crying and it wasn't any sort of cut.

"It's not that," I said quietly. "It's because it's the only photo we've got of Us Boys and Mum."

Paris picked up the photo and looked at it. "Is that really you?"

I nodded. "And Johnny."

She shrugged. "Tommo's not even in it."

Which isn't true, because he is actually inside Mum's tummy, but anyway, it made Tommo cry even louder. Which is when Johnny walked in and found us.

And Other Nan was wrong because Johnny swept up the glass and got Tommo a chocolate milk out of the fridge to cheer him up so he hasn't gone Off The Rails, at least not yet. Only that's when we smelled it.

At first Johnny thought I had farted and said, "Christ, Billy, that is minging." But I said it wasn't me, and Tommo said it wasn't him or Sonny. Paris said it couldn't be her because she's a girl, and Johnny said, "Who even are you?" and she said, "I'm Paris Potts, duh. Anyway, he who smelt it dealt it." Johnny said he hadn't dealt anything that bad, not ever, which is when I realised who had dealt it. I looked under the kitchen table, and there was the dog, and there was something else and all, because it wasn't just fart it had dealt. It was a massive poo.

Johnny didn't know which to be more cross about, the poo or the dog, but he decided the poo was the first thing to be tackled. He went to the shed and got Tommo's Bob the Builder spade, and scooped it up and put it in a plastic bag and put the bag in the bin. Only then we had a pooey spade.

Johnny held it out to me and said, "Your turn."

Which made Paris scream and go, "Omigod, that is the most disgusting thing, like, ever. Just throw the spade away as well."

Only that made Tommo's eyes go all wide and I thought he might start wailing again so, even though she was right about it being disgusting, I got some kitchen roll and some spray and cleaned the spade and the floor.

When all the poo was gone and Tommo said the spade passed the hygiene test, Johnny said, "Right, now do you want to explain why there's a stray dog in the house?"

I felt weird then, God. Because I knew you'd sent the dog, but Johnny doesn't believe in you. He says it's like believing in the tooth fairy, or Father Christmas. But then I remembered what Miss Merriott said about faith – that it's about believing even when other people say you're doolally.

"God sent it," I said. "I asked for it and God sent it so that Dad's heart will melt and he won't be cross all the time any more."

Johnny went quiet then, and stared at me dead hard, and I waited for him to shout, or tell me I'm bonkers. But in the end he just shook his head and said, "You'd have been better off asking God to make Big Sue disappear." Because Big Sue is the one organising the strike, which is making Dad worried, which is making him shouty in the first place.

Then Tommo said, "You said God's not real, though, Johnny, so how could he do that?"

And Sonny said, "Nice one."

But Johnny said, "Whatever." And then, "Shut up."

Tommo said, "No you shut up."

Johnny said, "Don't be a knob."

But Tommo didn't repeat that because of the swear jar.

Instead, Johnny looked at the dog again, and said, "You are so going to be in Big Trouble when Dad gets home."

Tommo said, "YOU'RE so going to be in Big Trouble for being out all day."

Which I agreed with.

But Johnny didn't. He said, "If you DARE tell Dad I was out I will literally kill you."

And Paris said, "Literally? Like with a gun or something?" Because Miss Merriott is always telling us off for saying "literally" when we don't mean it.

But Johnny did mean it. He shouted, "Literally. With my bare hands. All right?"

Only it wasn't all right, because then Tommo started crying about being killed by bare hands, and Paris and Sonny started arguing over whether that was even possible, and I saw that the dog, who we'd sort of forgotten about even though we were arguing over it, had slunk into a corner and was trembling again.

"Ssshhh," I said. And amazingly everyone did *ssshhh*. I went over to the dog, and sat next to it and stroked it and said "ssshhh" to it too. And so did Paris, and so did Sonny and Tommo.

"It's all right," I said. "It'll all be all right, you'll

see." Which I didn't know was true but it's just what you have to say, isn't it?

Then I remembered something. "And anyway," I said. "Dad will be too busy having his heart melted to be cross."

"As long as it doesn't do another poo," said Paris.

"It only did a poo because it was scared," said Tommo. "I saw it on *Dog Rescuers*."

"So we won't shout any more," I said.

Johnny said, "Fine. But if anyone asks, it was your idea."

I said, "Fine."

And Paris said, "Can I come back and see the dog again?"

And I said, "I suppose."

And she said, "Nice one."

Then Johnny walked Paris and Sonny home because it was their teatime, and came back with fish and chips and mushy peas. The dog had some too, only not the peas, which it tried but didn't like, or the pickled egg, which Johnny said would make its poo smell worse than earlier. Now the dog is back in the tent ready to surprise Dad when he gets back, and me and Tommo are going to bed soon too, only in our own beds because the dog didn't seem keen on us sleeping in the tent.

So mainly I wanted to say thank you. Because I asked for a dog and now I've got one and so Dad's heart is going to melt and he'll stop going bonkers and want to be home with Us Boys all the time. And also, because of the dog, Paris Potts is going to come round mine again. Which I didn't ask for, and I know she's a girl and a bit loud and sometimes annoying, but it's actually a bit incredible.

Night then.

Tuesday March 15th
11 a.m.

Dear God,

Dad's heart didn't melt.

He got home extra late last night because of his shift running over. That meant his heart couldn't have melted until today anyway because he went straight to bed. Only this morning, when I opened my eyes from being asleep, there was Dad in our bedroom saying, "Jesus, Billy, what the flaming hell is that?"

I looked to see what the flaming hell it was,

and it was the dog on the end of my bed all curled up like a delicate dragon, only one that smelled of wee. At first I was all warm and syrupy inside like when you've eaten porridge, because the dog must believe in me and know I'm a friend not an enemy. But then Tommo woke up and he was cross that the dog had slept on my bed and not his.

Dad said, "Why is there a dog on anyone's bed at all?"

I said, "God sent it."

Dad gave me a look that seemed like he didn't think you had sent it and said, "Right." Then he marched off to Johnny's room and dragged him back in (only not for at least five minutes because it takes Johnny a long time to get out of bed in the morning, sometimes an hour).

Johnny looked dead angry when he came in, because of being woken up and because he thought I'd told on him, and also a bit mad because his hair was all standing up in a mess, and his eyes were hardly open. So I quickly said, "It was all my idea, honest, and God's."

Dad said, "I don't care whose idea it was, it was a stupid one."

I said, "God's not stupid."

Dad said, "He is if he never washes his animals or feeds them."

I said, "He does! God loves his animals. Even the dog. Even though it smells."

Which is when Johnny said, "The dog doesn't belong to God, you knob. It belongs to the Pattersons."

And I said, "Does NOT!"

And he said, "DOES. It's got a racing number on its ear if you don't believe me, look."

And I did look, and he was right, and I said, "Oh."

Tommo said, "Fergal Patterson's definitely Off The Rails. He once flushed Nirmal Singh's head down the loo."

I thought Johnny would say, "That's a lie." But

he didn't, he said, "Yeah, well Nirmal Singh once buried Robbie Cox in the high-jump pit up to his neck, so he's Off The Rails and all."

Dad said, "You're all flaming Off The Rails if you ask me." Then he looked right at Johnny and said, "Are you sure it's from the Pattersons?"

Johnny nodded.

I said, "How?"

He said, "They've got loads up there. Fergal said. They race them."

Dad said, "Right, well you can flaming well take it back there then."

But there was no way I was taking the dog back, because what if they flushed *its* head down the loo for running away? And I said so. Only then I said something else, something that I shouldn't have but I was angry inside, like there was this hot and red and mean thing in my chest and arms, that made me want to hit things or say bad stuff, and what I said was: "Mum would have let us keep it."

Dad's face went funny then and I thought

maybe he might shout at me, but he didn't. He just closed his eyes, and then said quietly, "She wouldn't have, Billy. She was allergic, remember?"

I did remember then. I remembered that I asked and asked and asked for a puppy and in the end Mum took me round her friend Dawn's house to see Roxy her Labrador and by the end of the visit she'd sneezed a bazillion times and her nose was red and so were her eyes. And I think we all remembered, even Tommo because I'd told him about it, because we all went quiet, which made me feel even worse inside.

Dad took a deep breath and made a sort of speech. I could tell he was still cross, even though he used an indoor voice. He said, "This is what's going to happen. Either you and Johnny take the dog back to the Pattersons or I'll take it down the police station myself, seeing as I've got to go there anyway because *someone* nicked Tommo's scooter and your bike last night because *someone* left the shed door open, which is what I was coming up here to tell you in the first place, and which is the last thing I need with work like it is right now."

I really thought I might faint then, and Tommo too because he went all pale and ghost-like. But he just started crying instead, so Dad said he was sorry Tommo had lost the scooter, but it was a lesson in taking care of things. Only Tommo yelled that he didn't care about the scooter, he cared about the dog.

And I realised I didn't care about my bike either. All I cared about was keeping the dog. I held on to it then, with my arms round its neck, so I could feel it all warm, and feel its heart going pitter-patter like it had mice inside it. And it felt feeble and alone and like it needed a friend. And that friend was me.

"I can't take it back," I said.

Dad said, "Yes you can, and you will. I don't have time for this. Tommo can go to Mrs Potts, but I need to be able to trust you two, do you understand?"

Which I didn't, not really. I think he could tell because then he said, "Or your flaming Nan's going to get her way."

And I said, "Nice Nan?"

And he said, "No, Other Nan."

And then I thought of what that would mean. You know, me and Tommo moving in with her and not living with Dad or Johnny any more. And I had to let go of the dog and run to the bathroom in case I was sick, but I wasn't, I just coughed a bit.

When I got back, Tommo was getting dressed for Sonny's and Dad had taken the dog downstairs for breakfast. I thought that meant maybe he'd changed his mind but he hadn't. He'd just given it a bowl of water and two cold sausages and said that was its lot, and we had until he got home to sort it or else.

"Or else" sounded bad, like worse even than moving in with Other Nan, so me and Johnny are going to take it in a minute.

I don't really understand why you would do

that, God. Send a dog, even a smelly one from the Pattersons, and then make it go away again. Other Nan says you move in mysterious ways. But this is so mysterious I don't even think Sherlock could solve it.

6 p.m.

We didn't mean to do the bad thing.

It started off just like Dad wanted. We made a lead out of mine and Tommo's dressing-gown belts and got the dog to walk down the garden and along our road, which is called Elland Street. It's my favourite road in our town because of our house but also because, above all the red roofs and the chimneys and the satellite dishes, you can see the hills that have been there since possibly even the dinosaurs. And that reminds me that the world is bigger than one street.

The dog seemed to like it too, because it sniffed the air and looked up at the hills and then at me, and then it trotted beside me all the way to the corner. Only when we turned on to Gartside Road, which has cars and a zebra crossing and Mrs Beasley's shop, its legs started trembling again. Then it made a yowling noise and tried to climb through Mr Hegarty's hydrangeas, which Johnny said wasn't a good idea because Mr Hegarty threatens to call the police for anything untoward. For instance the time Tommo kept using his front wall as a tightrope, and the time Dad told him to mind his own business when he said Dad was raising hooligans. Like Dad said, we're not hooligans, we're just boys.

As we were trying to yank the dog out of the hedge, a car stopped and it was Little Sue, who works with Dad and who Tommo wants to be our stepmum, only Little Sue has a girlfriend so that's not likely to happen. Anyway, Little Sue said it looked like we were having bother.

Johnny said, "No we're not."

And I said, "Yes we are."

And Johnny elbowed me in the ribs which

made me say, "Ow!" which is when the dog burst out of the hydrangeas all covered in leaves and stuff.

And Little Sue said, "Oh, I didn't know You Boys had a dog."

And I said, "We don't."

And Little Sue said, "Funny, because that looks like a greyhound to me. Don't you, you look just like a greyhound." Which was to the dog, not me, obviously.

And Johnny said, "It's from the Pattersons, must've run away."

And Little Sue sucked breath through her teeth and said, "Who can blame it. Well, rather you than me." Only then she must've changed her mind because she said, "Tell you what, hop in, and I'll drop you off at the end of the lane."

And so we did.

Surprisingly the dog seemed quite keen on getting into the car, which is a black Ford Fiesta Zetec. It climbed into the back and sat between me and Johnny, with its legs across my lap all hard and bony with the hair worn off in places. I was wondering why it was worn off, and also why it's OK that we call Little Sue "Little Sue" even to her face but it's not OK to call Big Sue "Big Sue" ever, except at home, when the dog put its head on my lap and looked at me with sad eyes. It was like it had all the worries of the world in its head and it was too much for its skinny shoulders. And I felt my own eyes prickle then, like there was something in them, and I think maybe it was love. Then I felt properly bad that we were taking it back, even though Dad said it was that or the police.

Then Sue stopped the car and we were there. I looked up the lane at the buildings, all low and corrugated like cardboard, only made of rusty metal. I said a prayer that Little Sue would say, "Let's just stay in here, shall we, and I'll persuade your dad to keep the dog and we can all live happily ever after." But she didn't say that. She said, "Here we are, then. I can wait if you like. Run you back home."

Johnny said no thanks because he might chat to Fergal for a bit so Sue said, "Okey dokey," and so we got out, and she drove off. At the time I was sad because of my prayer not coming true, but now I'm glad Sue left. Because otherwise we'd never have got away with what happened next.

The dog absolutely did not want to walk up the lane. I tried begging it, saying "come on" and pulling it with the lead, but that just made its legs shake and its eyes bulge even bigger and I was scared I would choke it. So we tried pushing it instead but it was surprisingly strong for a thin dog and all that happened is that its claws dragged through the gravel before it sat right backwards on top of me, which made me sit down on the ground with the dog on top of me, which made me and Johnny laugh. Only then we remembered that this wasn't funny, not one bit.

I said, "We'll have to carry it."

And Johnny said, "Are you mad?"

And I said, "Well you come up with a better idea."

Only he couldn't, so in the end he just said, "You owe me big time." And then he picked up the dog in his arms and started walking. I scrambled to my feet and caught up and held the dog's paws in my hand to help, and also to show the dog that I was still its friend.

The dog didn't mind being carried, which is amazing really, especially with Johnny huffing and swearing. But it did mind when we got to the yard, and it could hear all the other dogs in the corrugated metal barns yapping and scuffling. It started to scrabble, and so Johnny dropped it on the ground. It slunk behind me, pushing itself against my legs so hard I thought I'd fall over again, but I pushed back a bit, so that we were holding each other up.

Johnny said, "I suppose I'd better ring then."

I could tell he didn't want to, but he went to the

house, which wasn't metal, but still looked grey and gravelly and mean. I said another prayer then, that the door wouldn't open, and this time it came true because Johnny rang another three times, and knocked on the window, and even texted Fergal, but no one answered anything.

I said, "Where are they?"

Johnny said, "How the hell should I know."

So I said, "Leia will know." Because Leia knows everything, like which stars in the sky are which, and how to draw a realistic skull.

It turned out I was right because Johnny rang her and said some stuff, which I didn't hear because I put my hands over my ears in case it was rude or love, but then he hung up and said, "They're in Lanzarote."

So I said, "Now what?"

Johnny said, "I don't know. There must be a manager or something. Someone to feed them. So let's just shove it back in a barn and then leave."

I said, "We can't do that."

Johnny said, "We don't have a choice, do we."

He marched up to a barn, and pulled back the lock and opened the door. Then something weird happened, which is that he shut the door again straight away and when he looked back he was dead pale, like Leia when she's done her zombie make-up.

I said, "What?"

He said, "You don't want to know."

But I did want to know, so I patted the dog and said, "I'll be right back." Then I walked up to the door and opened it, just like Johnny. And then I knew why he'd closed it again. Because it was bad, God. Badder than you can imagine. Think of, say, a place where all the dogs are packed in together like battery chickens. And they all smell of Dead Grandpa and are sad and trembling and barking. Then try to imagine it a bit worse. That's what it was like.

Me and Johnny looked at each other then, for a long time.

"Shall we go home?" I said in a quiet voice.

Johnny's voice was quiet too. He said, "What about the dog?"

I said, "We did what Dad asked. We brought it back. If it follows us home, that's not our fault."

Johnny said, "OK then."

So we left.

After ten steps I looked round, and there was the dog, trotting after us. It trotted all the way down the lane, along the main road, past Mrs Beasley's on Gartside Road and round the corner on to Elland Street. And I knew that you were watching us, God, because I did prayers all the way that no one would spot us, and they didn't. Not one person said a word, and nor did the dog. It didn't bark once, not like the ones back at the kennels. Not even when a taxi honked dead loudly. And then we got home.

So that's the bad thing we did. Only we did it for a good cause so it's only half bad I think. We're keeping the dog in the shed until we work out what to do. It's big enough and it has a window so the dog has daylight, plus whoever took the bike and the scooter didn't take any of the other stuff, for instance the old lawnmower or the jam jars with nails in or the baby clothes, so the dog will have interesting things to look at.

Johnny said Dad's bound to find out. I said he wouldn't because of the not barking thing. Also Dad will probably be on shift until the weekend and by then the dog will be trained to sit and lie down and do tricks maybe. Plus dogs are therapeutic so it might cheer Dad up once it's started behaving.

Johnny said, "Where did you hear that?"

I said, "Telly."

Johnny fixed the door then while I tidied up the clothes bags and made a nest for the dog to sleep on. Then I sat down with it and told it that it was our dog now, and this was its home for a bit.

"I wish I could have brought all your friends," I said. "But there's not really the room in here. But I'll work on that, I promise."

It seemed to understand, because it gave a sigh and put its head on my lap again and looked up and I saw all sorts in its eyes. I could see a reflection of the shelves and the sky through the window, and I could see me too. I was in its head like it was in mine. I kissed it then, between its ears, which I know is not a manly thing to do, plus possibly not hygienic, but it felt good, God.

I felt good.

When Dad got home he said, "Who fixed the shed?" and Johnny said he had, and Dad said, "Nice one, Johnny Rockets, although not much point now the flaming thing's empty." Johnny just shrugged, which is amazing, because normally he goes bonkers when Dad calls him Johnny Rockets.

It'll be amazing if we get through the next few days without Dad finding out, though, especially now Tommo knows.

I said, "Listen. The dog came home after all, but don't tell Dad."

Johnny said, "Fat chance." Because Tommo told on Johnny that time he took a fiver out of the swear jar for some Red Bull and a Mars bar.

Tommo said, "I won't tell!"

Johnny said, "If you do, you're for it."

Tommo said, "What's 'it'?"

Johnny said, "You don't want to know."

Tommo said, "I do."

But Johnny said, "Just bloody swear to secrecy."

And Tommo nodded then, because swearing to secrecy is dead exciting, like in films.

Tommo made the swear up for us all. "I totally promise not to let on about the dog. Especially not to Mrs Beasley from the shop, who is a beaky cow." Which is true, she is.

Then we each said it in turn, or most of it. Tommo added about ten other people not to tell including Other Nan, which was actually a dead good plan as there is no way she would approve because she says dogs are unhygienic and time-consuming.

So if you could help Tommo keep that promise that would be really good.

9 p.m.

Dad came in just now to say good night and also sorry about the dog but that we'd done the right thing taking it back. Little Sue had told him what good boys we were when she came into work, so he was proud of us. I felt sick then, because of the secret. Dad must've seen because he said, "I'm sorry, Billy. I know you liked that dog."

I thought about all the other dogs then, the ones we left behind, and I thought, *I like them too.* I wanted to tell him so much I was scared the words might burst out, because even though he shouts a lot he's a good person and a lover of animals (except slow-worms and pangolins, which he says are just weird) so maybe he could help us to rescue them. But then I remembered I hadn't even rescued one yet, so maybe I'd better not blab. Instead I said, "Do you think we can have a dog of our own one day?"

Dad tried to smile, but it was a fake one, the kind where you're not smiling on the inside. "One day, Billy," he said. "But I just don't have the time or money. Not right now. Not with the job and You Boys. And not with the flaming strike. Christ, we'll all be eating dog food at this rate."

I said, "Can't I just have beans on toast?"

It must've come out panicked because Dad said, "I didn't mean it. It won't be that bad. But ... things are hard. Do you understand?"

I said I did even though I didn't. And he said "good boy" like I was a dog. Then he ruffled my hair and went downstairs for *Storage Wars*.

But I still feel bad.

But also good. Because the dog is right there, at the bottom of the garden. I can see it from here, God. Not the dog, I mean, just the shed, but I know it's lying there with a bowl of water and a tennis ball to chew and its own bed made of Tommo's baby blanket.

And right there, I have a miracle. Not as impressive as the thing you did with the loaves and fishes maybe. But still, a miracle.

Night.

Wednesday March 16th

8 p.m.

Dear God,

Tommo didn't keep the secret.

Dad dropped him round the Potts's on his way to work and he was supposed to be there until me and Johnny picked him up at teatime, only by half past ten he was back in our garden with Sonny and Paris. They were all chewing bubblegum and wanting to see the dog.

The shed was a bit cramped with all of us in it but Johnny said it was that or they could go home, because if the neighbours saw us Dad might find out and we wouldn't have a dog any more. So we squidged in, all except Johnny who went to play loud music on his own.

The dog didn't seem to mind the squidge, though, because Tommo and Sonny took turns stroking it and giving it Cheetos to eat, which are cheesy snacks that make your fingers orange, and also your nose if you are a dog. They also gave it a packet of cheese slices, some leftover chicken curry, and a hard-boiled egg that was meant for sandwiches for lunch. It swallowed the egg in one and we all cheered. And I said, "Well done, Dog."

Paris said, "Dog? Dog's not a name."

And Tommo said, "What *is* its name?"

I said I didn't know, and that maybe it didn't have one, or just a long racing one. Paris said we should give it one, and I agreed, because a name would make it feel like our dog, not the Pattersons', and also help Dad to bond with it.

So we took turns thinking up ideas.

I said "Dave" because it's our uncle's name.

Only Paris said, "You can't call a dog Dave, it's got no dignity."

And Tommo said, "Besides, she's a girl dog. You can't call a girl Dave."

I said, "How do you know?"

He said, "Because it doesn't have a penis, it has a vagina, which is where babies come out."

Which is when I realised he'd been reading Dad's midwife books again. Dad will go bonkers if he finds out because last time he read them, Tommo used the word "testicle" in the corner shop and Mrs Beasley heard and stopped letting us have credit.

Anyway, then Sonny said "Taylor as in Swift" and Paris said "Jessie as in J" only we looked at the dog and it didn't look like a Taylor or a Jessie. Or a Wolverine or an Elsa or any of the other names we came up with.

In the end I said, "Can't we just call her Dog?"

Paris said, "A dog called Dog? That's not very imaginative."

Sonny agreed. He said Miss Hooley, who's his and Tommo's teacher, would go mad because "dog" isn't a wow word, which means dead interesting. But I said what's not interesting about Dog? No one could argue with that, so Dog it is. Then Sonny and Tommo went outside to practise doing tightrope for Brimley's Got Talent, only not on an actual tightrope, just on our washing line on the ground. Sonny says he's going to be the First Human Boy ever to walk the tightrope while also eating a packet of chocolate peanuts. Only he kept wobbling so Paris confiscated the peanuts so me and her could eat them in the shed.

It was just me and her then, which was weird. But not horrible. Not at first, anyway.

She said, "Have you got a talent for the show?"

I shrugged, because I've thought of loads of things but I'm not good enough at any of them, not enough to be The Incredible Billy Wild anyway, and not enough to tell Paris Potts about. I could feel my face get hot and I knew it was going red so I said, "What about you? Shouldn't you be practising your singing?"

She said, "I don't need to. I'm pitch perfect. That means all the notes are exactly the right ones. Do you want to hear?"

I really did, only I didn't want to sound like an eejit, so I said, "If you want," which is what Johnny says when he's trying to play it cool with Leia, which is mad if you ask me, because she knows he likes her.

Anyway, she sang a line of "Price Tag" and it was surprisingly good, then she stopped and said, "That's your lot."

So I said, "Why?"

She said, "I'm saving my voice for the big day. You've got to be careful with it, like it's made of eggshell. I saw it on *X Factor*."

I said, "You should audition for that."

But she said she's not old enough for four

years and eight months, and Simon Cowell will probably be too old by then to even be on telly.

I didn't know what to say to that so I held out a chocolate peanut for Dog. Paris snatched it out of my hand.

I said, "It's not like it's the last one. There's still some in the packet."

She said, "Duh, I know that. But chocolate is poison for dogs. It could kill her."

I said, "Just one chocolate peanut?"

She said, "Just one."

So I gave the packet back to Paris and she put it in her pocket to be safe in case Dog tried to snatch it, because she is quite good at snatching things she thinks are dead interesting. For instance the cheese sandwiches we made for lunch and also Tommo's strawberry milk. And then when Johnny came to say goodbye and also, "Don't do anything stupid," because he was going round to Leia's, Dog sniffed his pocket and tried to get something out of there too, only it was cigarettes.

Tommo said, "Smoking's for fools," which is what Dad says, because it makes your insides black and your willy not work if you have one.

But Johnny just said, "Whatever," which is ten pence in the swear jar but none of us bothered to say it because he'll only take it out again and spend it on cigarettes. Tommo says it's a vicious circle.

No one knew what to do then. Sonny and Tommo had given up tightrope walking because it's too hard, and now they are going to be the First Human Boys to do something else instead. Sonny wants to be the First Human Boy to jump through a hoop of fire on a dog. But Dog wouldn't even come to me when I told her to so she's hardly likely to jump through a hoop, especially not one on fire and especially not with Sonny on her back. She's too thin anyway. It's like she hasn't eaten for years. Every time she sees food she makes a whimpering noise so we give it to her. Only not chocolate. I know that now.

Owning a dog is a very responsible thing.

It's not a talent, or anything that would make me incredible, but I do want to be good at it. Because if I show I can be responsible Dad might let us keep her. That's what he said when Tommo wanted a hamster. Only then Tommo got his head stuck in the rails of Dad's bed which Dad said wasn't responsible at all, it was bloody stupid. That should've been fifty pence in the swear jar, but Dad had to saw the rails to let Tommo's head out and now his bed looks weird so we let him off.

Anyway, God, thanks for letting us have Dog. And for Johnny getting back in time to open the cans and heat up the meatballs before Tommo tried it. And for Paris warning me about the chocolate.

And especially thank you for Dad not finding out. At least not until Dog is brilliant and I am responsible. Which will probably be by tomorrow.

Night-night.

Thursday March 17th

11 a.m.

Sonny and Tommo have decided what they're going to do. They're going to be the First Human Boys to do somersaults off a top bunk bed at once. I said they were wasting their time because there was no way Dad would let them take the beds to the village hall, which is where the talent show is. But Tommo said it was important to think positively in life and then you will be rewarded by positive things happening – it's his new philosophy. I asked where he'd read that and he said *Chat* magazine.

He is right, though – I need to be positive about Dog. All I have to do is be responsible and train her excellently and then Dad's heart will melt and he will love her. And maybe then he'll love Us Boys a bit more too.

I don't see how he can't love her, really. Sometimes when I look at her, for instance when she lies with her front legs crossed and her head on her legs and her eyes looking up at me, the love is so fiery and bright it feels like my chest might burst open with it. Even though she smells, and has no fur on one side of her back leg because she's always chewing at it and like Tommo says her teeth leave a lot to be desired.

So that's what I'm doing. While Sonny and Tommo do tricks, and Johnny stares at Leia's boobs in his bedroom, I'm going to be responsible and do training with Dog.

7 p.m.

It turns out that training a dog isn't as easy as you might think.

I didn't start off with a difficult trick, I thought I'd just go with something simple first, like "sit", and build up from there. But when I said "sit" Dog didn't sit. She didn't even move an inch. I tried to push her bottom down to help but she just wriggled out from under my fingers. Then I thought, *Maybe she doesn't like sitting*, so I tried "lie down" instead, and I even showed her what to do. I lay down on the floor right beside her. But she just climbed on top of me and licked my face, which was nice, but not the point. So I pushed her off.

"Come on," I pleaded. "You've got to help! You've got to be good! Otherwise Dad's heart won't melt and he'll make you go back to the Pattersons where . . ." I couldn't quite finish that thought, as I could feel myself panicking, and I knew I needed to try something else. So I thought, *Maybe her talent is in retrieving things, like Labradors*, and I threw things for her like the tennis ball, and a beanbag frog and Tommo's broken Buzz Lightyear, but she just looked at me like I was mad.

"You're rubbish," I shouted at her then. "You're the most rubbish dog in the whole world."

Dog flinched then and I felt terrible. So I crouched down and stroked her and said sorry. "You're not rubbish," I told her. "Just that, it would be really good if you could do what I ask so that Dad loves you and you can stay." But when I said "sit" again she just wandered off and started chewing a sock, which is when Paris showed up.

"What's up with you?" she said.

I said, "Nothing."

She said, "Were you crying?"

I said, "As if," and wiped my face really quick, and that's when I saw the pram. "What's that?" I asked.

"It's a pram, duh," Paris said.

"Duh, I know that," I said. "But why have you got it?"

"It's for you," she said.

"I won't fit in it," I said. "And anyway, why would I want to?"

"Not you," she said. "Dog. It's so we can take her for a walk. We put her in and wheel her up to the Rec. That way no one will know what we're up to."

I was sick of training and I didn't have any better ideas, so that's what we did. We got Sonny and Tommo down from the bedroom, lifted Dog up and got her in the pram. She didn't mind as much as I thought she would, although that might be because Sonny put three custard creams on the pillow for her. Then we wheeled her out the gate and round the corner and right down the road to the Rec.

And it was amazing, God. The Rec is massive so we went over to the side far away from the bit with swings, where there was no one we knew and it's just grass. Then we lifted Dog out and put her on the ground.

At first she didn't really know what was what. She sort of hopped a bit and then looked back in the pram in case she'd missed a biscuit. But then a big gust of wind blew and it's like it blew excitement right into Dog because her ears pricked up and she sniffed the wind and then she was off.

Tommo and Sonny said, "Blimey."

Paris said, "Omigod!"

But I didn't say anything. I think all my words had gone with Dog. Have you ever seen a greyhound run, God? It's incredible. She just went with her head down and her back legs up, like she was flying, whirling in all sorts of circles, then there was a bird noise, a crow maybe, and she stopped . . . and then she was off again, charging to where it had come from. I got scared then, because I thought, *What if she ran away for good?* I called her name, "Dog, Dog, Dog!" And that's when it happened. She stopped and sniffed the wind again and looked around as if she was just checking it was me calling, and then she came trotting back with her tongue lolling out and pushed her nose into my hand so I would stroke her. I wanted to cry again then, but I didn't. Instead I crouched down and buried my nose in her fur and sniffed the fresh air smell on her.

"Good Dog," I said.

"Good Billy," Paris said. "She listened to you."

"Do you think?" I asked.

Paris nodded. "Try it again."

So I did, I let go of her, and she was off again, until I called her name, "Dog, Dog," and she came running back, once, twice and then three times.

But then I let her do it a fourth time. And that's when it went wrong.

She'd run off to the dead conker tree and all of a sudden she was rolling around underneath it, like she was the happiest dog alive. Then she came trotting back, only as soon as she got close

I smelled it, and it was bad, worse than her own poo.

It was fox poo. Tommo said so. He'd seen them talking about it on *Countryfile*, about how it was the smelliest of all the animal poos because of all the junk food and meat foxes eat.

So I said, "Now what?"

And Paris said, "We have to wash her. In the bath with proper shampoo. Because then she'll be glossy too and your dad will love her more."

I said, "It's what's on the inside that counts," because Miss Merriott is always reminding us.

Tommo said, "Dad might not know that."

And I thought maybe Tommo and Paris were right. Because I know you love everything, God, even wasps and dogs covered in fox poo, but for human people it's usually easier to love something that's clean on the outside and smells of, say, pine-fresh bubble bath rather than Dead Grandpa.

So that's what we did. We stuck her back in the pram, only on top of a plastic bag that Sonny found near the bins so that the poo didn't rub off, then we wheeled her home and gave her a bath.

It started out OK. Better than OK even, because when we lifted Dog into the bath she didn't seem to mind at all. In fact she liked the blue water and drank a bit of it until I stopped her in case of more bad poo. And then we shampooed her using Johnny's special shampoo which guarantees your hair will glimmer and also smells of coconut. Paris made some hair for her out of foam and put it on her head and we took photos of her on Paris's iPhone so she could see herself. Although Dog seemed more interested in eating the phone than looking, so we had to stop. Then it was time to rinse her off and that's when the first bad thing happened.

As soon as I turned the shower attachment on, Dog went mad and tried to escape only the bath is slippery so she kept falling over. Paris and Tommo and Sonny tried to hold her down but she was all slippery too and she slipped right out of their hands and scrabbled over the side of the bath and across the floor. I was so shocked I forgot I was holding the shower attachment and I showered Sonny and Tommo and Paris and also the bathroom floor and walls and even the ceiling at one point. Tommo turned the tap off then but we'd made a massive mess. But that's not even the worst bit. The worst bit is that once me and Paris had got Dog back into the shed, Tommo and Sonny went back to doing their talent so now the beds are wet too. Also Tommo's somersaults are not all they could be and in one he accidentally landed on a model car which was surprisingly sharp and now he has a cut on his leg. He started crying so I yelled for Johnny to stop staring at boobs and do something useful for once, only when he came out something was wrong with him too because he had a massive purple mark on his neck.

Sonny said, "I knew it. She IS a vampire."

This is because Sonny doesn't like Leia. He reckons she looks like a vampire because of all the black lipstick and black clothes. Tommo said vampires aren't real, they're only on telly and in America and anyway she's named after a princess in *Star Wars* so what's not to like. If anything, I don't know what Leia sees in Johnny. He's always moody and he smokes and I know for a fact he farts really loudly. She must have a high tolerance for smells and idiots.

Anyway, then Leia came in and she had a massive purple mark too which made Sonny's eyes open really wide and he said, "Omigod, your brother's a vampire and all."

Johnny said, "No I'm flaming not, you knob."

And even though Tommo was crying he still said, "That's fifty pence in the swear jar."

Which Johnny didn't agree with because he said, "And who's going to make me?"

And it turns out no one was, because no one said anything except Paris who said, "That's not a vampire bite, that's a lovebite. They're a sign of passion and also broken blood veins in your neck, so really it's just a bruise, which is not very exotic when you think about it."

And Sonny said, "It's also kind of gross."

And then Leia said "whatever" and Tommo yelled "ten pence!" and Johnny said "seriously, knob off" and that's when Dad walked in.

He wasn't even supposed to be home yet, which I said, but that made it worse, because he was all, "Oh thanks a bunch, Billy boy. I manage to get off shift early and this is my welcome home." So I felt bad. But not as bad as I did when Dad saw Tommo's leg.

He said, "Christ on a bike, what happened?" (Which is factually inaccurate because there weren't bicycles in the Bible, as I'm sure you know, God.)

So I said he fell off the bed because of trying hard to be in the talent show.

Dad said none of us seemed to have any talent in the bloody brain department, especially not Tommo, which made Tommo cry even harder because Other Nan is always saying he is the brains of the family. So then Dad said sorry and checked Tommo's leg and it's not broken and the cut's not even that deep. It's superficial, which means on the surface only, just like Dog was superficially unloveable. But even though we've made Dog *look* more loveable now, and even though she came back when I called her name, she still needs a lot more training, especially in the poo department. We've run out of wet wipes now, what with all the scraping and cleaning up. I've added them to the shopping list, as well as more Cheetos, chocolate milk and mini sausages. You should ask for all those in heaven, God. I reckon you'd like them, especially the Cheetos.

Anyway, the point is, I've still not told Dad about Dog. Because of the training, and because he sent Paris and Sonny and Leia home, and he sent Johnny to his room to cover his neck up, and me and Tommo had to mop up the bathroom.

Plus it's going to be straight to bed after tea with no TV and no pudding, so he's clearly not in a heart-melty mood.

Night.

Friday March 18th

11 a.m.

Dear God,

When I got up I saw that Dad had crossed Cheetos, chocolate milk and mini sausages off the shopping list. I asked why and he said snacks like that aren't value for money and you get more for your nutrition and calories with things that don't come out of packets, like bananas and a piece of toast and normal milk-flavoured milk. I think Little Sue's been at him again for taking in leftover pizza and crisps and Nutella sandwiches for his packed lunch, even though Nutella has hazelnuts in which are nutritious.

Tommo's going to go mad when he gets back from Sonny's. He hates milk that tastes of normal and Johnny hates anything that isn't out of a packet. I don't think Dog's going to be too pleased either. Although she did eat two pieces of toast for breakfast. One with Marmite for mains and one with jam for pudding. Only I'm not sure that toast is that nutritious for dogs because she's done three poos already this morning and they were not normal ones. They were like when you've eaten, say, a lot of curry or maybe some bad fish. I had to get the Bob the Builder spade out again and rinse it under the outside tap, but the smell is still there.

I don't suppose you have to worry about poo in heaven, do you? Although what happens to the nectar and ambrosia that you drink? I read that on Google. Though I don't suppose you have Google up there either, which is a shame. You can learn anything on Google. Like the names of all the people who've ever played for Leeds United, or what wasps are for, or even how many different kinds of monkey there are, and there's one that has a long spindly finger for getting weevils out of holes, which I think is dead interesting and so does Tommo. Although you probably know all that anyway what with being omniscient, which means all-knowing. I'd like to be omniscient but I'm not. Like I don't know why Johnny smokes even though he knows it's bad. Or why Dad works so much even though it makes him cross and us sad. Or why you took Mum away from us.

And for once Google hasn't got the answers either.

4 p.m.

Leia says there's definitely something wrong with Dog.

She came round again this afternoon so her and Johnny could sit in his bedroom and play music about death, only she stopped off in the shed just when I was scraping up the seventh bad poo of the day.

Johnny said Dad was going to get suspicious soon because of the smell and the bits lying around that I couldn't scrape. I said we could pretend it was a cat but Johnny said no cat did poo that disgusting and also why would it scrape up its own poo? Leia asked what we were feeding her so I told her what Dog had had today which was:

- The two pieces of toast
- A slice of pepperoni pizza left over from tea which we were allowed because Dad had already bought it before the junk food ban and it's waste not want not
- Five Jammie Dodgers, which are biscuits with red sticky stuff in a hole in the middle and are also waste not want not
- A corn on the cob and a carrot for vitamins

Leia said there was the problem, right there, because Dog's diet was all wrong. And I said but what about the vitamins from the carrot, and she said it's not vitamins that's the problem it's the no protein and all the bad stuff from the junk. Leia says Dog needs proper dog food twice a day and no snacks and also some proper exercise. Sonny said, "How do you know?" And she said because her aunt has a Labradoodle called Marilyn so she knows all about dogs.

I have to buy proper dog food for Dog. But Dad didn't leave any money out for takeaway and I've only got fifty-six pence left out of my birthday money because of buying some football stickers and a book about the solar system. Which I said to Johnny, but he said he hasn't got much money either and I said, "Because of cigarettes?" And he said, "Because of none of your business. Try the swear jar."

So I did and it had twenty-two pounds and eighty-nine pence in it, which is a lot of swearing.

But I said I couldn't take money that isn't mine, because it's wrong. Johnny said technically some of it is mine for the swears I've done, but I've only done two "whatevers" and a "bloody hell" and that's only seventy pence. Besides, when it gets to thirty pounds Dad's going to take me and Tommo to Legoland. Johnny said that was unfair seeing as he does most of the swearing and doesn't get the benefit but Tommo said if Johnny keeps taking money back out then we'll be too old for Legoland by the time we get to thirty pounds anyway.

So I've taken ten pounds out. I'm not sure how much dog food that will get but as long as it's enough until Saturday when Dad's heart melts it'll be all right. And also I promise I'll pay it back when it's my next birthday, unless I get a WHSmith token because I don't think Legoland will take those.

Being a dog owner is expensive. Expensive and responsible.

9 p.m.

Buying dog food in Brimley is harder than you think. Or at least it is when you're not supposed to have a dog.

Me and Paris went to the corner shop while Johnny and Leia watched Tommo and Sonny do their talent show act, which is now being the First Human Boys to juggle a plate, an orange and a tin of spaghetti hoops. Only they won't be because they keep dropping them. When we walked in the bells jangled and Mrs Beasley looked up and said, "Oh you again, Paris Potts. I've got my beady eye on you."

So we went down the grocery aisle where she could still see us but couldn't hear us because she doesn't have beady *ears*, and Paris explained that Mrs Beasley is still cross because once Paris knocked over the bargain biscuit display because her and Sonny were arguing over who was best: Iron Man or Wolverine, which she said was Wolverine and I agreed.

Anyway, we found the dog food and there were four kinds: three in tins and one which is just biscuits. Paris said we should get one of each, just in case Dog is a picky eater. I pointed out that Dog had eaten a half-chewed tuna sandwich once and a peanut that fell out of Sonny's mouth so she was hardly picky. In the end we got the biscuits and four tins of chicken flavour Pedigree Chum because chicken is Dog's favourite crisp flavour even more than prawn cocktail.

Only when we got to the till, Mrs Beasley looked at us with her beady eye and said, "I didn't know you had a dog, Billy Wild."

I felt my legs go weird then, like all the blood evaporated and the bones shrivelled and they were just skin and air, and without really thinking I said, "I don't have a dog."

Only that made Mrs Beasley pull an even worse face and she said, "Well, I hope it's not for you then. I saw that on the news. Children having to eat dog food because it's cheaper. Not right, it isn't. Poor mites."

And I remembered what Dad had said, and my legs went even weirder and then it just came out – another lie, like I'd sicked it up. "It's not for our dog, and we're not poor mites, either. It's for the dogs at the shelter. We're doing a good deed, so there."

And I know it was another lie but it was for a good cause again which is nutrition for Dog and also not having Mrs Beasley round to check we're eating properly. Which we will be now the junk food is being banned. And it was worth it because when we got back Dog liked her new food, and we only let her have the amount it said on the box, even though she asked for more by looking at me with her big sad eyes. But I was firm and responsible and said, "Not until the morning or you'll poo weird again." And that was that.

Next time I'll go to Discount Deals, though, because it's new girls on the tills in there and they're mostly just talking to each other about telly and their boyfriends, who are always doing the wrong thing, and I have no idea why they stay with them if they are as bad as they say. Girls are strange. Probably because of the eestro-something. But I like at least two of them anyway i.e. Leia and now Paris too.

Leia and Johnny are taking Dog for a walk every evening. Johnny didn't want to at first but she said if he doesn't then she'll go on a kissing ban, which Tommo said would be a good thing because actually ten seconds of kissing can spread eighty million bacteria which is unhygienic. But Johnny didn't agree because he said, "Oh, bloody hell. All right then."

And it's good because Leia can pretend it's, say, her aunt's dog if anyone asks. Plus Mrs Beasley already doesn't like Leia because of being from Poland even though she was actually born in Bolton, which is dead English, and Mrs Beasley was born on the Isle of Man, which isn't.

Leia wasn't lying when she said she knew all about dogs. She told us that when greyhounds are too old, they get called the "Good-For-Nowts" and they're killed with a bolt in the head, or dumped all ill and broken at the side of the road, sometimes with the tips of their ears sliced off so you can't tell what their racing number was so they can't be traced. I checked on Google and it's true. It made me think about the dogs at the Pattersons' kennels, all packed in and smelling. And about Dog too. Even though she still has her racing number in her ear, she was so thin and shaky when she came to us that maybe she thought she was a Good-For-Nowt and they were going to dump her or put a bolt through her head. And when I thought about that I thought you couldn't be omniscient, God. Because if you did know about that you would stop it, wouldn't you?

If I was omniscient, or even just incredible, that's what I'd do.

Night then.

Saturday March 19th

11 a.m.

Dear God,

I had a nightmare last night about the bolt going into all the greyhounds' heads and their ears being chopped off. I woke up and I was crying and Dad was there, and he was saying, "It's fine, Billy, it's fine, it's just a dream." But then he looked at my glow-in-the-dark alarm clock and said, "Jesus."

I said, "What?"

He said, "I've got to be at work in three hours."

I said, "Sorry."

Dad said, "Can you just try dreaming about, say, a chocolate factory, or something?"

I said I'd try. But I accidentally started to invent a lot of different kinds of chocolate instead of going to sleep, and then before I knew it Karol was honking outside and Dad was stomping off so I got up and went on the computer. I don't know what the point of Google SafeSearch is if it stops pictures of ladies' boobs coming up but doesn't stop pictures of dead dogs. What's scary about a boob? Although I also don't see what's so interesting about them either. Johnny does, though. He is always staring at boobs. Mainly Leia's. They're up in his bedroom right now and he is probably just staring at her boobs. Or possibly her eyebrows. They're really black but some of it's make-up and once they washed off in the rain.

Sonny and Tommo are wearing make-up too. It's because Paris says she might be a make-up artist when she grows up. Her mum says it's important to have something useful to fall back on after the singing. She asked if she could do me too but I said "No way," because what if someone saw me and Seamus Patterson found out about it? I said Sonny and Tommo are bonkers for letting her because now they have red lips and cheeks, and their eyelids are totally multi-coloured and mad-looking but they don't care. I said, "No way am I going out in public with you."

Tommo said, "Well no way am I going out with you."

So they're staying in the tent all day working out what they're going to be the First Human Boys to do and me and Paris are staying in the garden with Dog. That way we should all stay out of trouble, so that Dad will be in a better mood when he gets home.

5 p.m.

It is amazing how much trouble you can get in even when you don't do anything untoward. Because me and Paris did stay in the garden with Dog and we got her to poo on the grass behind the shed when she needed to go, which is easily scrapable and doesn't need wet wipes. And Tommo and Sonny did stay in the tent and didn't try to be the First Human Boys to do anything mad at all. Only something else stayed in the tent too and that's where the trouble started.

It was Dad who noticed it. He was checking Tommo's leg when he got home after lunch and said why was it all red around the outside, had Tommo been pulling at the plaster, because if he'd been told once he'd been told a thousand times to leave it alone. But Tommo said he'd not been pulling at the plaster, he'd been scratching the bites.

And Dad said, "What bites?"

And Tommo said, "These ones." And showed him, and there were twenty-three of them, all on his ankles.

And I said that was funny because I'd got bites too and there must be a mosquito in the room.

Nice Nan says Spain is full of them and she is always covered in mozzie bites unless she puts on her special cream.

Only Dad said, "It's March, and this is Brimley not flaming Benidorm, and these aren't mozzie bites, these are from fleas, Billy, fleas."

I went quiet then and so did Tommo because we both knew where the fleas must've come from. Only so did Dad, because he said, "That bloody dog, Billy!"

No one mentioned the swear jar because Tommo was too busy scratching and I was too busy feeling sick because I thought Dad had found out about Dog and was going to march straight out to the shed and drag her out and send her back to the Pattersons to have a bolt in her head. Only instead he marched straight to the tent which is still up in our bedroom and lifted up the flap and stuck his head in.

Then he said, "Flaming hell, will you look at this."

So we stuck our heads in too, in a line from top to bottom. I did a gasp noise and Tommo said, "Flaming hell," just like Dad, because inside the orange tent were lots of little black dots sproinging up and down and crawling around.

"Fleas," I said. "Thousands of them."

Dad said, "Well, thirty or so maybe, but yes, fleas. For crying out loud, as if I haven't got enough to deal with, with your Aunty Geena still stuck in Kettering and a strike meeting here tonight and all. I'll have to cancel that now, won't I."

I felt bad, then, which is the only reason I said it, and I know I should have asked you first, but it just sort of came out. I said, "God will fix it."

Dad said, "God's not real, Billy."

So I said, "Is too real."

Dad leaned towards me then, so close I could see the red veins in his eyes and the lines on his forehead. He said, "Oh, really? You think there's a God, do you, Billy? Have you looked at the world lately? Or even at us? Have you thought about why we're in this mess?"

I shrugged at that because I haven't, if I'm honest.

Dad carried on. "If there was a God don't you think he'd maybe help us out once in a while? Don't you think he'd fix the strike, or send Geena back from the back of beyond, or . . . " He stopped then, and I knew he was thinking, "or send Mum back from heaven." And I wanted to hug him, only his face was still too scrunched up and he didn't look huggable.

Then Tommo piped up. He said, "Anyway, God might be a she."

But Dad said he didn't care if God was a one-legged elephant with a dragon's head and a monkey's arse, he or she or it was useless.

Then he dragged me and Tommo out, and yanked down the pop-up tent and tried to put it away, only it popped up several times which annoyed him even more and also sent several fleas springing out into our room which we tried to catch but couldn't because they are surprisingly quick. In the end Dad just squidged the tent together and stamped downstairs with Us Boys behind him and threw it out the back door and then he marched back upstairs with Us Boys behind him.

"Now what?" asked Tommo.

Dad said, "Now you pick up all the crap off your floor and I wash all the flaming bedding and clothes, only I'll have to take it down the launderette to tumble because it's going to pee it down later which just goes to show there's no sodding God."

Then he closed his eyes, and put his hand over them, and did some deep breaths and said, "Sorry. I'm sorry for shouting. But can you just do as I asked." So we did, picked up the crap, which isn't crap, it's stuff like Transformers and Nerf darts and Pokemon stickers but Dad doesn't understand because he's old.

I was just picking up the last Nerf dart and thinking how cool it would be if you did really look like that one-legged elephant thing, God, when I heard the yell from the kitchen. And that's when I remembered about the swear jar money which is what Dad always uses when we need the tumble driers. I was scared my Cheerios were going to come back up when Dad yelled again, only the yell wasn't for me, it was for Johnny.

Johnny opened his door and said, "What now?" in a bad mood because he's a teenager and they don't like to get up until the afternoon or be asked to do things. It's biological.

Dad said, "Get down here."

Johnny sighed and did get down there, and so did me and Tommo just to see. I was right about the swear jar because Dad was holding it and saying, "Do you want to explain this? Or shall I just assume it's all gone up in a puff of cigarette smoke."

Me and Tommo gasped then because we didn't know Dad knew that Johnny smoked.

Johnny said, "I don't smoke."

But Dad wasn't having any of it. He said, "I wasn't born yesterday. I can smell it on you."

Then Johnny did a massive shrug.

Dad said, "Really? That's it? Christ, I'm working my backside off trying to keep this family afloat and you're trying to kill yourself and take the rest of us under in the process."

I could see Johnny getting annoyed and I had to take a deep breath and hold it because I was scared Johnny was going to tell on me. Only instead he said, "Yeah, so I took the money. But it wasn't for fags, OK? It was for a present for Leia."

I know it was a lie which is bad overall but it was really impressive because normally Johnny can't think of things quick like that. Also, it was a lie that saved me because Dad said, "Well it's coming straight out of your allowance, kid. And I want you off the bloody cancer sticks too, all right."

And Johnny said, "Fine," only it sounded like it wasn't.

And Dad said, "Good," only it sounded like it wasn't that either.

Then Johnny marched back upstairs and Dad said, "And you two can do something useful while you're at it. Get your shoes on, we're going to the launderette."

I didn't want to go because I was worried about leaving Dog on her own, but I couldn't tell Dad that, so I just tried to send her a telepathic message not to worry and that I would be back later. Then we picked up a massive bag of wet clothes each, which are at least twice as heavy as dry clothes which Tommo found highly interesting and I found annoying, and we walked round the corner to Soap Stars.

Normally I like the launderette. It's warm and smells of washing powder and there are usually old ladies in there who give me and Tommo slightly fluffy Fruit Polos and then talk about their illnesses to each other. Only today it was just me and Tommo and Dad, and he wasn't talking at all except to say, "We can't go on like this. There's going to be some changes. Starting tomorrow. Do you understand?"

And we just nodded, even though we didn't understand at all.

When we got home Dad went inside to phone someone, probably about the strike meeting which he says will have to be at Little Sue's now. So me and Tommo went to the shed on gang business, which is what we told Dad only really it was to see Dog.

I gave her some biscuits and I told her about Dad being angry but that it's probably only because he misses Mum which is why he's still got her perfume in a bottle in his drawer and her clothes in the wardrobe. He thinks we don't know about that but we do. Then I told Dog that I miss Mum too and that she would have liked Mum.

I said, "It's hard to remember everything, Dog, because it's quite a long time ago now."

Tommo said, "As long as my age so six years and four months."

And I said, "Six years and four months. But I can remember that she smelled like blue Lenor fabric conditioner so when we have that it makes me think of her. Also she liked green Fruit Pastilles and she always ate mine for me because I really only like red and orange."

Tommo said, "I like green. Because I have inherited the green gene."

Even though I know there probably isn't a green gene, I didn't say anything. Instead I told Dog about the best memory of all. "Whenever she had a glass of wine, for instance at Christmas, or on Saturday nights, she sang "Danny Boy" because that's Dad's name and it made him cry. It goes like this."

And I sang then, just the first two lines. And Dog's ears stuck right up, like she was listening really hard. "I'm not as good as Mum," I said then. "So I don't do it much, plus I don't want to see Dad cry any more."

When I said that, Dog sniffed right in my ear,

and licked me, like she knew it had been hard to say out loud.

Then Tommo said, "And she once ate too much beetroot and it made her wee go red and she thought she was dying, tell Dog about that." Because I've told him before and he likes that story best.

But I said, "Why don't you tell her?" And he did.

At the end, Tommo said, "Maybe we should get Dad a new one."

And I said, "New what?"

Tommo said, "A new mum for Us Boys. Then he won't be cross all the time, because someone else can make sandwiches and deal with fleas plus they would have the Woman's Touch."

I agreed, so we thought about who it could be. And I said, how about Miss Merriott because she is kind and wise and also sent Seamus Patterson to the headmaster when he called me a rude name. But Dog sighed when I said that. So Tommo said how about Mrs Potts? Because she lets him and Sonny play out without ever worrying where they are. And wear shoes on the sofa, and even have pudding for main course sometimes. Although she would have to do something about her eyebrows because they are drawn-on like Leia's, only not very well because she always looks a bit surprised. I said she'd have to do something about her boyfriend too. Tommo said she hasn't got one and I said, "Has!" And he said, "Hasn't!" And I said, "Has, because Paris told me, so there."

She has and all. He's called Nog Bates and is a postman and also Ultimate Frisbee Champion for the North West region. She got him online six months ago like Nice Nan did with Maurice. Then Tommo said maybe that's what the changes are. Maybe Dad's got a girlfriend already off the computer and she's going to move in tomorrow, and our house will be like one of the ones on telly on the DIY shows only after they've done all the changes instead of before, which is what it's like now. That made him happy and it made me happy too. Then Tommo said, "I'm tired of talking. I'm hungry." And I realised I was too, so I said we should go in. We gave Dog a hug and a kiss and another biscuit each, then we trooped up the path to the house.

When I got in, I realised that even though I was hungry, I wasn't tired of talking. Because there was someone else I wanted to talk to and that was Paris. Only I couldn't call her because my mobile is for emergencies only, so I texted her. It took ages because even though I've got spellcheck it got confused with "fleas" and "fleece" and also put the word "Johnnycakes" in for no reason at all.

Anyway, I did it in the end. I told her about Dad's maybe girlfriend, and also about the fleas which Dog still has because we found another load while we were stroking her, and killed them by squeezing them between our thumbnails like it said to on Google. About one minute later my phone beeped and it was Paris! She said she can get something for the fleas off her cousin Donna who works at Pet Sense which will put them right off Dog. And also that if Dad has got his girlfriend moving in then we'd better hope she hasn't got kids, or there will be all kinds of war going on over who is best and who gets what room and Dad will be even crosser than he is now.

So if you could make sure the new girlfriend has not had any children that would be really good, God. Also that she doesn't want any more because mine and Tommo's room is cramped already even with the floor all neat and tidy. Also I had a thought which was, *Wouldn't it be amazing if you could prove to Dad you do exist by refilling the swear jar or un-inventing fleas?*

Night.

Sunday March 20th
10 a.m.

Dear God,

Me and Tommo are dead excited about a new mum. We washed our faces and brushed our hair without arguing once and now Tommo is reading a book quietly and I'm talking to you also quietly because Dad still doesn't know about you. He doesn't know about Dog either which is a miracle. This is partly why we are excited because hiding Dog is getting harder and it is hardest of all when Dad is actually at home. For example, this morning he decided to mow the lawn, only that meant getting the lawnmower out of the shed, so I had to think really fast. What I said was, "But you can't because we need long grass for a school project!"

Dad said, "What for?"

I said, "For bees." Because Miss Merriott is always on about the bees and how important they are. "We need to grow wild flowers and then I have to count the bees."

Dad said, "If a bee stings you, you won't be so keen then."

I said if it did, I would be sad because the bee would die.

Dad shook his head and said, "Sometimes I wonder what goes on in your head, Billy Wild."

I said, "All sorts." Even though it is mainly Dog right now, but I couldn't tell him that.

He said, "Fine, it can grow until the end of the holidays, but then you'll be the one picking it all up and putting it into a sack, OK?"

I said, "OK." And did an invisible smile, because I knew Dog's secret had just been kept safe, at least until the new girlfriend moves in. And anyway, having the Woman's Touch will make Dad calm and happy because the house will always be neat and tidy and Us Boys will be neat and tidy as well and also better behaved. And then we can tell him about Dog.

Not yet, though. Because at the moment he is making a special lunch and it's shepherd's pie only with beef not lamb, because Tommo won't eat lambs because they smile at you. I told Dad it was actually called cottage pie if it has beef in, only Dad says he'll call it what he flaming likes, thank you very much. So it is clear he is not calm and happy yet.

Anyway, I'll tell you what she's like after lunch or maybe this evening because I expect she'll want to take Us Boys out for a treat or maybe play Kerplunk with us, which is what Nog Bates did with Paris last Saturday, which is why she doesn't mind him so much.

So bye for now. ☺ (That's called a smiley. It means I'm extra happy because I am about to meet the answer to my prayer!)

7 p.m.

☹ That's the opposite of a smiley. It means I am absolutely the opposite of extra happy and you know why as well.

I don't understand. Why did you send Other Nan to us? She's not the answer to anybody's prayer, at least no one normal. And worst of all you're letting her stay all week to look after Us Boys while Dad's at work. That will mean no more crisp sandwiches for lunch, no more sliding down the stairs on the tray with the painted fruits on it and absolutely no more spending all day in the shed with Dog. Other Nan says she's got all sorts of interesting things planned but I bet they're not.

Johnny went bonkers when Other Nan was in the loo, which is usually a long time on account of her bowels, which means bottom. He said he didn't need babysitting, he was fourteen not four. Only Dad said if Johnny had been better at babysitting in the first place then Other Nan wouldn't have needed to come.

Johnny said, "I'm not being paid so why should I do it?"

Dad said, "Jesus, I don't know, Johnny. Because that's what family's for?"

But Johnny said, "Babysitting isn't my responsibility, it's yours. You shouldn't have taken all those shifts."

So Dad said, "Well the least you could do is set an example."

I said, "It's OK, I'll never smoke because I want my willy to work." And Tommo said it too.

Johnny said, "It's not even me you should be worrying about." And he looked at me then. And I knew he meant about Dog. And I was really worried that our Time Was Up. But luckily that's when Tommo went mad at everyone for saying he was a baby which he says he's not and also there's no actual law about having to have babysitters, he checked on Google. By then Other Nan had finished with her tricky bowels and was back at the table for pudding so no one said anything else. Although we probably could have done if we'd wanted, because Other Nan wears a hearing aid and she only turns it on when she fancies. Even when it is on if you whisper, say, "Poo bum willy," she can't hear you even one bit. I know that for a fact because Tommo tried it.

Johnny's still cross, though. Because of Dad saying Other Nan being here is all his fault, and because it means Leia won't be allowed round all the time so he won't be able to stare at her boobs, and also because it means he has to sleep on the sofa so Other Nan can have his room. Other Nan wasn't too keen either but Dad said it was that or she could bed down with Us Boys and she said she didn't fancy the fleas, thank you very much, so Johnny's room it is.

Worst of all, none of us got to see Dog until five o'clock and by then she was starving so we had to say sorry about a hundred times and give her extra massive kisses. Plus she'd done a poo and a wee because of not being able to get out, but in the corner like she'd held on as long as she could and she knew it was wrong. So I cleared it up with the spade and put it in the dustbin. Nan was at the back door when I did it and asked what I was up to so I said I found a cat poo and I was tidying it. She said I was a good boy and gave me a Murray Mint, so then I felt bad for not liking Other Nan that much.

But not for long because then Johnny said he might not be able to walk Dog tonight because of Other Nan having an eye beadier than Mrs Beasley's so now I feel bad for Dog instead. We'll have to make sure she gets double walking tomorrow because it's important for dogs like greyhounds to get a lot of exercise. Running is in their blood, sort of like watching *Storage Wars* and *The One Show* are in mine.

I've texted Paris to see if she has any ideas because she is quite practical when you get to know her. In fact it's one of her distinct talents like singing and doing make-up that looks like you're not wearing any. Which I said was pointless but she said that's because I'm not a girl so I don't understand, and actually most women are always wearing make-up but they make you think they're not because of the importance of being natural. I didn't say anything after that because it sounded mad only I didn't like to tell her.

Anyway, I hope Paris comes up with an answer and also that she can get the flea stuff off her cousin Donna because there are still several in our bedroom. Tommo says maybe we could catch them and then he and Sonny could be the First Human Boys with their own flea circus. But I looked it up on Google and flea circuses don't have actual fleas in, it's just a trick.

Today has been highly disappointing. There's no new mum and Other Nan's here for almost a whole week and Dog pooed in the shed. Also it's raining. But I'm being positive for Tommo's sake and he says the sun will come out tomorrow. Well actually he is singing it, because it's a song from *Annie* the musical and he thinks his talent might be the First Human Boy to play Little Orphan Annie. It isn't. But I haven't told him that because of being positive.

I wish you'd show us all what our talents are, God. But especially me. That way I might stand a chance of being incredible.

Or at least making Other Nan less minty.

Night.

Monday March 21st
1 p.m.

Dear God,

Other Nan has only been in the house for a day and already she's found nine things that are wrong with Us Boys. They are:

1. We do not know the meaning of "be quiet".
2. We do not know the meaning of "wait your turn".
3. We do not know enough Bible facts

because we haven't been reading *The Bumper Book of Bible Stories* that she got us for Christmas two years ago. I said we had read them but sometimes it is hard to remember which are Bible stories and which are from *The Mammoth Book of Myth and Fairytale.* Other Nan did not agree.

4. We do not understand the importance of doing chores, for instance washing up and drying up and tidying up. I wanted to point out how good me and Tommo are at doing all the chores for Dog, like feeding her and changing her water and picking up her poo but I couldn't for obvious reasons so I dried the cereal bowls instead, and Tommo stood on a chair and put them back in the cupboard and only one got chipped.
5. We do not wash our faces or our hands or our private parts enough. Tommo said he

had a bath two days ago and so his willy is sparkling clean. He offered to show Other Nan but she said no.

6. We eat too much sugar.
7. We do not eat enough vegetables.
8. We spend too much time on the computer and not enough reading books or playing out and our brains will shrivel up and so will our legs and then we'll be sorry. Tommo said you could learn a lot from the Internet, for example how to make cake-in-a-mug in the microwave which Dad did once and it worked and we had cake for breakfast for a week, only Other Nan did not seem keen on that idea because of point 6.
9. We do not know the meaning of the word "stop".

Johnny does not know the meaning of morning because he is still asleep on the sofa.

Other Nan says it is unhygienic and also ungodly so Tommo asked why but she didn't have an answer for that. She just said, "Go brush your teeth or they'll rot away and fall out like your Great Uncle Brian's." Great Uncle Brian is Other Nan's brother and it is clear he is the black sheep of the family on Mum's side, which means the odd one out. He is a Very Bad Man because a) all his teeth fell out b) he married a Wanton Woman called Beverley Lannister who made him move to Grimsby and c) he put his feet on the table a lot.

Also Other Nan is not happy about me and Tommo spending all day in the shed. We told her it was our gang hut like in the olden days, because she is dead keen on things from the olden days. She said she'll think about it when we get back from the park which is where we're going in a minute to get some fresh air and stretch our legs. I said the air in the garden is quite fresh but Other Nan did not agree.

On the plus side this afternoon can only be an improvement. Other Nan thinks so too.

9 p.m.

Other Nan was right for once, God. This afternoon was the most excellent afternoon since you sent Dog to the shed in the first place and I'll tell you why.

What happened is that when we got back from the park Paris and Sonny were sitting on the back door steps.

Other Nan said, "And who might those two unlikely characters be?"

Tommo said, "They are actually very likely and it's Paris and Sonny and they're in our gang."

Other Nan said, "Why have they got a big pram?"

I said, "I don't know," which was a lie, but I think this is one of those situations where the truth would have been worse.

Other Nan's lips went very thin and she said,

"Playing with prams just encourages the wrong sort of girl to want babies."

And Paris heard that because we were at the back door by then and she said, "I don't want babies. It's my mum's."

And Sonny said, "I don't want babies either."

And you'd have thought Other Nan would be pleased about that at least but she said, "Well, if you think you're coming in the house you've got another thing coming. The floor will only just be dry from the mopping this morning." Then she looked at me. "And I bet That Brother of Yours has tramped around in his dirty boots since then so it'll need another wipe. Three boys is a lot of work. No wonder your dad can't cope."

I said, "He can cope."

But Other Nan didn't seem to hear me. She just said, "You can all go to your gang hut while I have a cup of tea and a sit-down."

*

So we did.

First of all, Paris gave Dog the special flea stuff she'd got off Donna, which was only a dot of something on her neck not a massive can of powder like Tommo had hoped. Then we bundled Dog into the pram again and took her to the Rec for a run.

And this time I wasn't scared at all when I let her go, I knew she'd come back when I called. And that's not all. Because when she got back to me, I said, "Good Dog. Now sit." And I pushed her on the bottom and this time she just did it. No sniffing, no licking, no trying to waggle out of it, she sat straight down.

And we were so happy because of how highly excellent it was that we started singing "Price Tag" by Jessie J, which is about how dancing is more important than money, and also "22" by Taylor Swift, which is about liking boys who look like bad news, which seems bonkers to me but Paris didn't think so. And I didn't even care that my voice isn't as good as Mum's, it just felt good to sing. Incredible even.

Anyway, that is when something incredible really did happen, which is that Dog joined in. I'm not even joking, God. Dog actually started to sing.

We'd just got to the bit in "22" about everything being miserable and magical at the same time, which I was thinking is sort of what living with Dad is like, when Dog made a noise from under her blanket – a sort of whine and a howl all at once, like a baby. At first I thought she was ill and so did the others so we stopped singing, only as soon as *we* stopped so did Dog.

And then Paris looked at me and I looked at her. It's like we were in each other's heads or something because I knew exactly what she was thinking and I was thinking it too, so we started singing again.

And so did Dog.

She sang the whole song with us in her howly dog voice. And then at the end we all clapped and gave her a pat. That's when Paris said it. She said, "This is it, Billy. This is our talent."

I said, "What talent?"

She said, "For the show, duh. We'll be the world's first boy-girl band with an actual singing dog."

I said, "What do you mean, 'we'?"

She said, "Me, you, the boys and Dog. We'll all do it together."

I felt my stomach jump then. Because that would mean being on stage in front of the whole village. And part of me imagined it, with everyone cheering for Dog, and the others, and me, The Incredible Billy Wild! But part of me thought, *What if we mess it up? And then everyone will laugh, plus we'll be in massive trouble with Dad*, which I said.

Paris said, "You don't get it. Your dad will be all, 'That is the coolest dog, like, ever.' Because everyone else will be saying that. And no one wants to be the odd one out."

I said, "Do you think so?"

She said, "A hundred and ten per cent."

Tommo said, "That's not actually possible, Dad said."

Paris said, "Is too."

Tommo said, "Is not."

Paris said, "Omigod, who cares?"

And Tommo didn't have anything to say to that. So Paris looked back at me and said, "But we still have to keep her secret until then, because otherwise spies might steal our idea and, say, get three dogs to sing."

I nodded.

"So is it a deal?"

I looked at her then, and she was smiling so wide at me that it was like the smile jumped on to my face. And it felt like there was nothing we couldn't do together. So I said, "Deal."

Tommo and Sonny went mad with excitement at that and started dancing round the pram singing and Dog joined in again and we were all singing like mad when we got back to the garden which is when we stopped and luckily so did Dog. Because there outside the shed was Other Nan without a coat on and looking all red in the face.

I felt like I did the time Miss Merriott caught me picking my nose and I thought she was going to say it out loud in front of the class only she didn't, she just shook her head. But Other Nan didn't just shake her head.

"Billy Wild," she shouted. "Where in the name of our holy father have you been?"

I said, "Down the park."

She said, "On your own?"

I said, "No, with Tommo and Sonny and Paris."

She said, "That's not what I meant and you know it."

Only I hadn't known it, but I didn't say that in case it made her worse.

She said, "You should have got me so I could come with you."

I said, "But you were having a sit-down."

And Tommo said, "And anyway, if you'd come out, Johnny would have been in on his own and what if Leia had come over and bitten him again?"

Other Nan got flummoxed at that and said, "Well next time you tell me, do you understand?" And we nodded to say we did understand. Then she looked at Paris and Sonny and said, "Isn't it time you two were off? Your mother will be worried sick about you."

Sonny said, "I wouldn't bet on it."

But Other Nan doesn't believe in betting, or ghosts or aromatherapy which she says are made up, so she just said, "Come along now, boys. We can have a nice game of cards and some oatcakes."

Tommo said, "Worst luck." Because he says oatcakes are made of cardboard.

Other Nan said, "I heard that, don't think I didn't. That's no pudding for you tonight."

Tommo went red and walked into the house before he got any more things banned or confiscated, but I said, "Just going to say goodbye to Paris and check the shed's locked, Nan."

And she said, "Good boy, Billy." Which made me feel a bit bad because I wasn't really being a good boy, I was putting Dog away and giving her her tea and also talking to Paris.

Paris said, "What do you think?"

I stroked Dog's head as she ate her tea and said, "About what?"

Paris said, "Duh. Brimley's Got Talent. Me and you and the boys and Dog."

I thought about that. "If we did win, we might get on telly. And then we might win loads of money and Dad could give up work and also shouting so much."

She did a face then, which was a silent "duh", which meant I was right. And then a smile, and I smiled back, because I'd just come up with a plan.

Then her and Sonny wheeled the pram off out

the gate, and I said goodbye to Dog, and locked the door carefully, and walked back up the path to the house.

So today has been excellent after all. Because I won cards four times. And because the oatcakes had ginger flavour in so they weren't as cardboardy as usual. But mainly because I might actually be The Incredible Billy Wild, which would mean Mum wasn't lying after all.

And it's all because of Dog.

Dog is the best thing that's ever happened to me, God. Remember when I said how happy she looked, running? That's how I feel right now. I feel so happy I could howl with it. I won't because Other Nan wouldn't like it. But in my head I am howling to Taylor Swift and so is Paris four roads away and so is Dog down there at the bottom of the garden. And you know what? I think she'll be the best thing that ever happened to Dad too, once he finds out.

Now we've got our talent, that is.

Your ways weren't so mysterious today, God. I wish you were like that all the time. Then more people might believe in you.

Night.

Tuesday March 22nd
8 p.m.

Dear God,

You know how yesterday was excellent? Well today was the opposite. Paris says it's called *yin and yang* and is about balancing the universe out and is highly spiritual, only I don't feel highly spiritual at all. I just feel cross and tired and so does everyone else and it is all down to Tommo's enormous brain.

What happened is that Dad left before breakfast so there was no interesting cereal, just brown toast, which Other Nan said was good for our bowels. Tommo said he didn't care about his bowels, he'd rather have cornflakes, only Other Nan did care. And she cared about a lot of other stuff too i.e. our eyes turning square from looking at screens all day and she decided we needed less being on Google and more Structured Activity. So she'd planned an outing to Duckett's Farm to see the lambs being born on account of it being Easter in a few days' time. Although I'm not sure what lambs have got to do with Jesus but Nan said I ask too many questions and to put on my anorak and a scarf because it's parky in the barn.

So I did. I also texted Paris to tell her we were out and couldn't rehearse or even look after Dog so could she let her out to do a poo and give her some food, only not too much because we're running out.

When I got back Other Nan had her hat on and her hands on her hips. "Get your coat on," she said to Johnny.

"I don't want to get my coat and I don't want to see lambs," he said. "I'm fourteen, not flaming four."

Other Nan said, "Sometimes it's hard to tell." Which is actually quite funny for Other Nan if you think about it. Tommo laughed but Johnny didn't see the funny side and stormed up to his room. Only then he remembered it wasn't his room at the moment, so he stormed to the bathroom instead and locked himself in.

In the end Other Nan said he could stew in his own juice and we went just the three of us. Only I think Other Nan wishes she'd left Tommo at home to stew and all now.

It started out OK, because actually it wasn't that parky in the barn because of all the sheep in there with their lambs who were jumping up and down a lot and also sucking your finger, which feels weird but nice. Then Tommo saw a sign that we were allowed to sit on the hay bales and hold a lamb and have photos taken for five pounds.

Other Nan said we could hold the lamb but not have photos, which the man with the camera said wasn't an option. Tommo said please, please, please to having a photo but other Nan still said no and why didn't we go to where the crowd of people was at the back of the barn, so we did.

When we got there there was a lot of *ooh*-ing and *aah*-ing. Me and Tommo wriggled to the front so we could see better and it was a lamb actually being born. Other Nan yanked on my anorak hood then and said we should come away because it wasn't nice. Tommo said he wasn't coming anywhere because this was the wonder of birth, which is what Dad is always going on about and getting tears in his eyes. Other Nan said there was nothing wondrous about seeing a lamb hanging out of "there". And that's when it all went really wrong because Tommo said, "It's not called 'there', it's called the vaginal canal. I read about it in a book."

I've been down a canal once, in Manchester.

It was brown and there was a dead pigeon and a shopping trolley in it. I didn't want to think about that being inside a sheep or a person, and I don't think Other Nan did either. She went all pale like a ghost Nan, and then bright red. Only Tommo didn't seem to notice. He was too busy talking to the man in overalls about the placenta, which is a thing inside a lady that the baby is attached to, and how it gets food to the baby and how in some countries they even eat it after it comes out because it is full of nutrients.

That was when Other Nan said it was time to go. She grabbed Tommo and pulled him outside, which I'm not surprised about because she won't eat McDonald's let alone placenta. Then she marched us back to the bus stop and we rode all the way back to Gartside Road with no one saying a word.

Then it got worse because Other Nan needed to buy some milk and some crackers from Mrs Beasley. I said I'd wait outside but Other Nan said,

"Not on your Nellie," which means the same as "no way" so me and Tommo had to go in. And I tried to be really quiet and unnoticeable but it is hard because of Mrs Beasley's beady eye and she spied me behind some Jammie Dodgers and said, "I thought I saw you, Billy Wild. No Paris Potts with you today, then?"

I said, "No," and Mrs Beasley said, "Good job too," which set Other Nan's ears wagging because even though she is a bit deaf she is always keen to hear other people's business.

She said, "Why's that?"

Mrs Beasley said, "She's trouble with a capital T, just like her mother."

I said, "Actually she's very kind and helpful."

But Mrs Beasley just tutted at that and said, "Pigs might fly."

And luckily Tommo didn't say about the thing he'd seen on the Internet which was a pig in an aeroplane, which meant pigs *could* technically fly. Mrs Beasley finished ringing up the milk and the packet of Ryvita so I was just thinking we could get out now any second when Mrs Beasley said it.

"No Pedigree Chum this time, Billy?" she said.

And I could hear my heart hammer like it was in my ears instead of my chest and my throat closed up to keep the sick and the words in.

Other Nan said, "Why would he buy dog food? He hasn't got a dog."

Mrs Beasley said, "For the dog shelter. Isn't that right, Billy?"

And all I could do was nod because of my closed-up throat.

Other Nan looked at me then. And I thought she was going to go bonkers like she did over Tommo and the canal but instead a magical thing happened – almost a miracle.

She said, "Run and get a couple of tins then, Billy."

And I could have said no because it wasn't for the dog shelter at all, and so it was kind of a lie. But it was still for a good cause, which was Dog, so I got a couple of tins – chicken because they're Dog's favourite – and I put them down on the counter with the milk and crackers and Other Nan got her purse out again and handed Mrs Beasley another five pound note.

And I looked at Tommo because that was the five pounds he wanted to spend on the lamb picture but he pretended to zip his mouth and throw away the key so I said, "Thanks," to her and to him. And then I went home with the two tins in a carrier bag and my throat a small bit opened up and my heart a small bit lifted.

And then at the house it lifted a little bit more, because I went to put the tins in the shed because I told Other Nan that was where I kept them, which isn't even a lie, and when I got there Paris was inside with Dog half lying across her lap and they were talking about make-up. Well, Paris was talking and Dog was just lying there with one ear up so she was mainly listening, I suppose.

Paris didn't stop when I came in, she just smiled

and carried on about how concealer is a girl's best friend especially after those late nights. So I shut the door carefully and sat down next to her and stroked Dog. The weird thing was it was kind of nice just listening to her talk about nothing and everything. It was sort of like I'm doing now. Only to a dog.

And then she told Dog an amazing thing. She said, "My mum's having another baby. Only not with our dad, but with Nog Bates."

I wanted to say all sorts of things then, about when the baby's due and what it will be called and also how Mrs Potts needs to eat sensibly and take moderate exercise, but then she changed subjects and it didn't feel like the right time to interrupt anyway. I knew Paris was talking to Dog because it made her feel better, just like talking to you makes me feel better, God. And then I thought something else – maybe she was even talking to me, because that made her feel better too. Even though I didn't know if it was true, it made me feel good, like I was helpful, and also worth talking to. It's sometimes hard to believe that in our house, what with all the shouting.

Anyway, after Paris had finished telling Dog about false-lash-effect mascara she got a piece of paper out of her pocket. It was the entry form for Brimley's Got Talent and on it she'd written: *The Famous Four and their Amazing Singing Dog.*

I said, "Is that us?"

She said, "Duh, obviously."

I said, "I like it. But it's quite long."

She said, "So?"

I said, "Well most famous bands are just two names like 'The something' or one name even, like 'Madonna'."

She said, "Well if you think you can do any better, Billy Wild, you come up with something."

So I thought. And first I came up with "The Famous Five" which is an actual book about four children and a dog, only Paris said the book people might sue us and we had to be original which is why she said Famous Four in the first place, duh. So I thought again and I remembered about another book called *The Starlight Barking*, which Miss Merriott read to us in class. It's about an extra-terrestrial dog, which means from another planet, and the dog was called Sirius which is also the name of a star in the sky which is also known as the Dog Star. Which is what I said.

Dog Star.

Amazingly Paris agreed and she rubbed out what she'd written. Over the top she wrote *Dogstar* as one word because she said it was more memorable like that. She knows a lot about talent shows and being memorable so I said OK.

Then we sang "22" really quietly. Dog howled and so we stopped because of Other Nan, and also because we were laughing so much, and I said, "You are a dog star, Dog," and put my arms round her neck. Paris agreed and did the same. And that was the nicest I've felt in a long time, God. Probably since me and Dad and Tommo and Johnny all watched *Frozen* and Dad let me stick my head under his arm where it fits just right and we all pretended to hate the film, especially Dad, but when Elsa sang "Let It Go" I looked and his eyes were wet and so I squeezed him and he squeezed me back.

That's what this felt like. And it's hard to explain but it's sort of like being safe. I think that's maybe what grown-up love feels like, only I like this kind better because there's no biting of necks and no babies.

Then the safe feeling went because Other Nan yelled for me to come in because it was starting to rain.

I said, "I'd better go if I don't want my guts for garters."

Paris said, "What even are garters?"

I said, "I don't know but I don't think they're good."

She said, "I'll Google it and text you later then."

And I said, "OK. Bye then."

Then I gave her a hug. Dog, I mean. Not Paris.

Because that is the sort of thing girls do, not me. Then it was back to taking my shoes off and eating with my mouth shut and opening it wide when I'm talking so I don't mumble. If you write down all of Other Nan's rules there'd be about a hundred of them, maybe even a thousand. I can see why Mum liked Dad now – because he hardly has any compared to that.

That's the problem, though. Because when Dad got in from work Other Nan started at him about the no rules and why Tommo was allowed to read unsuitable material about vaginal canals, only she didn't say that, she said "lady parts". She said it was clear the boy had his mother's brains and that they weren't being stretched at our school and he'd be better off at St Ignatius. That's the school where Mum went when she was little, but it's miles away.

Dad said, "He's not even in the catchment so you can drop that idea now."

Other Nan said, "If he lived with me he would be."

And that's why no one is talking to anyone any more and why today is the opposite of highly excellent. If I were looking for light at the end of the tunnel I suppose I would say that Paris talking to Dog and our new band name were it. But they're also part of the lies I've been telling to Dad and Other Nan and even though I know it's for a good cause, it still makes me feel bad so they're not really light at the end of the tunnel at all.

Other Nan says Dad should be trying harder to teach Us Boys right from wrong. But it's hard to tell the difference sometimes and if I'm honest you're not very clear about it either. Like in the Bible it says it's wrong to covet thy neighbour's bull which means to want something you haven't got. But what if you've got nothing and your neighbour has everything and is mean and won't share? What do you do then?

You should work on that, God. Maybe add a bit to the small print for these sort of circumstances. Dad says the truth is always in the small print.

Night.

PS I forgot to tell you that Paris texted to say that garters are bits of elastic for keeping ladies' stockings up in the olden days. So I definitely don't want my guts to be used for that, or anything else really.

Wednesday March 23rd
8 p.m.

Dear God,

It hasn't stopped raining since last night. And I know Other Nan says rain is a mixed blessing because it means the plants grow but it makes walking annoying, but Other Nan is wrong. It's mainly just bad.

At first I didn't mind so much, because she let us go on Google for an hour while we waited for it to dry up. Then when it didn't dry up she let us build an air-raid shelter out of the sofa cushions and Dad's bedspread, because Tommo said it was educational because they are doing World War Two at school and because Other Nan loves talking about the war and the Blitz spirit which is when everyone was happy in the face of disaster.

Tommo said, "But you weren't even born until 1944, how do you know?"

Other Nan said she was well aware of when she was born, thank you very much, and then she made us take the shelter down because she needed the sofa cushions back because the green chair is too hard. Tommo said that wasn't the Blitz spirit and Other Nan said he didn't know he was born only Tommo said, "Duh, yes I do," which is true but Other Nan sent him to our room anyway.

Then for lunch Other Nan made corned beef salad which is my sixth worst lunch and Tommo's fourth worst although it is still better than sardines on toast and anything with swede in. Johnny said he'd just have the salad because of being vegetarian and Other Nan said we should be grateful for what we're given and there are a lot of orphans and African children who would chop off their arm for corned beef salad. Tommo said if they did they'd be mad because they'd die and also not be able to eat the salad anyway because of the bleeding and not being able to pick up a fork. Other Nan said in that case he'd not mind missing pudding and she'd send it to a grateful orphan instead. He said, "Fine," because pudding was yoghurt which he doesn't like either and Johnny said it would go mouldy in the post or leak on the envelope so the orphan wouldn't be grateful anyway. That's when Other Nan told us to get out of her sight so she could have a lie-down. So we did. Johnny went round to Leia's and we went to the shed.

I texted Paris to come round but she said she couldn't because her mum's taking her and Sonny to TK Maxx on the industrial estate as a treat before the baby comes, plus they can buy cheap bibs so it's multitasking, which is very important for a woman. But then she said she had a new idea for a song for Dog and it's "Wings" by Little Mix, and me and Tommo should test it out. So we did. We found it on YouTube on my phone and played it to Dog and she started singing even without me and Tommo joining in. And I like the song even more than "22" because it's all about someone's mum telling them not to worry about what other people say, and just to fly with their wings only not real wings I think, just imaginary ones. Although having actual wings would be highly excellent.

The best bit is that the mum calls whoever is singing the song her "little butterfly" and I told Tommo then about how our mum used to call me and Johnny her "little soldiers" which made me feel safe but also like I was brave. Tommo said it wasn't fair that he didn't get to be little anything but then I remembered when he was inside Mum and she called him "Peanut". Tommo said that's not the same but then he said "Peanut" to himself quietly so I know he's happy about it really.

Then Other Nan shouted out the back door to come inside because the storm was getting worse and we'd catch our death of cold. Tommo was going to tell her that actually weather has no effect on viruses, for instance the common cold, but I said it was best to just do what she said without being too clever about it. Tommo said that was mad, because how can anyone be too clever, especially when Other Nan doesn't like Johnny or me so much because of *not* being so clever? I said they just can and he'd understand when he was older and to stop arguing.

It's not true anyway that I'm not so clever. It's me who came up with the plan to save Dog and help Dad love us more. And Mum said I was incredible, didn't she? The Incredible Billy Wild. And I know I haven't proved it yet, but I'm going to, me and Dog.

Once we were inside, Other Nan said we could

all watch a Wholesome Family Film so Tommo said *Star Wars* and I said *X-Men* and Other Nan said, "Not on your Nellie," and got a DVD out of her bag which she got off her friend Maureen from church and it was *The Wizard of Oz* and so that was that.

I don't know if you've ever seen *The Wizard of Oz*, God, but it's about a girl called Dorothy and her dog Toto, and a massive wind called a tornado blows them and their house all the way to another land which is called Oz. And it's actually a lot scarier than say *Star Wars* or *X-Men* because of The Wicked Witch of the West who Tommo whispered was a bit like Other Nan, only Other Nan said, "What was that?" and turned up her hearing aid so we were quiet after that and just concentrated on being wholesome.

Only then the flying monkeys turned up which were not at all wholesome and Tommo get really scared and Other Nan said it beggars belief that he can be matter-of-fact about a dead sheep but he's frightened of a made-up monkey. Tommo said it beggars belief that she wasn't frightened and Johnny who was back from Leia's and wearing a suspicious scarf said Tommo beggars belief full stop. Other Nan told him to put a pound in the swear jar, which he said also beggared belief but Other Nan said no it didn't, it was called "Tough Justice" and we could all do with a bit more of it and also if he didn't want to make it two pounds he had better belt up.

I didn't say I was frightened too but I was, so I was glad when Other Nan turned the film off and said we could watch *Countdown* instead. Tommo got a conundrum right and said, "Now that's what I call wholesome," and Other Nan tutted but Johnny and Tommo smiled. And even though I couldn't even get a four-letter word from all the letters, so did I.

So I'm trying to count my blessings like Other Nan is always telling me to and I can count:

- The new song that we can sing with Dog.
- Tommo liking being called Peanut.
- Tommo getting the conundrum right.

But the bad things are:

- Tommo being sent to his room for not knowing he was born.
- The corned beef salad.
- The yoghurt row.
- Johnny's scarf.
- The Tough Justice.

Which is two more than the good things so it doesn't really add up. Plus Dad is stuck at work because the next shift midwife can't get to the hospital because a tree has fallen into the road and the storm is getting worse and Dog hasn't had any exercise at all today. So on the whole I'm really worried.

I just thought I'd let you know in case you could think of some ways to fix it while I'm asleep.

Night.

11 p.m.

The storm is so bad it's woken me and Tommo up. At least Tommo says it's the storm but I think it might be the flying monkeys in his case. Anyway, Other Nan had to come up and let him snuggle and he asked her to sing "These Are a Few of My Favourite Things" which is what they sing during the thunderstorm in *The Sound of Music* which is his third favourite film and his first favourite musical. Only Other Nan said she didn't know that one and sang "Onward, Christian Soldiers" instead which Tommo didn't know and I didn't like. You probably do, though. Know it and like it, I mean. The funny thing was it was quite nice all being in one room, all snuggled up on Tommo's bunk. Other Nan said it was Blitz spirit and I understood it then. Though I wouldn't want to be in the war just to have it.

Tommo fell asleep in the end and Other Nan went back to bed but I'm still awake because of the film. Not because of the witch or the monkeys but because what if the wind turns into a tornado and whisks Dog and the shed into the air and miles away like Toto? Plus she must be worried in there all on her own with no one to snuggle with or sing "Wings" or "These Are a Few of My Favourite Things" or even "Onward Christian Soldiers". And I know she'll be wanting to put her head on my lap. And when I think of that, and of how close we are to the talent show and to Dad winning all the money and his heart melting, and me being The Incredible Billy Wild and the crowd cheering, it makes my chest all tight and my legs sort of itchy with needing to go outside.

So please, please, God, make the storm stop. I promise I won't ask for anything else again if you could just do this one thing. And I know you can because you sent the floods to Noah and then took them away again.

I'll even say "amen" if you want.

Amen.

See? I said it. So now you have to do it.

Thursday March 24th

4 a.m.

Maybe the wind was so loud you couldn't hear. Or maybe you had other stuff to do. Or maybe you just can't do miracles at all.

Because you didn't stop the storm.

You made it get worse.

In the end I had to go out. I didn't have a choice, did I. Not if I wanted to check Dog was safe.

And she wasn't.

I had to creep out of our room without waking Tommo and past Other Nan in Johnny's room and then past Johnny on the sofa and all. I thought the noise of my heart would wake him up because it was so loud in my chest and ears, but it didn't. And nor did the sound of me pulling on my coat and wellies and nor did the creak and click of the back door opening and closing.

The garden was madly windy. Normally me and Tommo would have said it was brilliant being blown around like leaves, but in the middle of the night with all the rain being blown as well it's no fun at all. When I finally got to the shed and opened the door Dog was backed into the corner whimpering like she had been the day she first arrived, all thin legs and trembling. But when she saw me she bounded forward and pushed her nose into my tummy and hands and I did a sob – a loud one – because of being so happy she was alive, but it was carried away on the wind so no one heard except me and Dog.

I sat down with her then in her nest of baby clothes and we snuggled up like me and Tommo and Other Nan did when we were singing "Onward Christian Soldiers". And then I knew what I had to do. I had to sing. I started out with that one but Dog didn't like it so I tried "Wings" again and she howled a bit but not as loud or long as usual. And even though I was sort of glad because of not waking Other Nan up I was also worried because that's not like Dog. I held her tighter then and said, "It'll all be OK, I promise," which is what Dad always says when I'm being sick or if I've hurt my leg or when I used to miss Mum. And even though it's not always true you do feel better for a minute.

It wasn't true this time. Because all of a sudden there was a massive *whoosh* of wind and part of the roof just flew off and I could hear it clattering down Elland Street. And then the wind and the rain were in the shed all swirling around and rattling jars and making babygrows fly in the air and Dog hated it. I was just thinking it couldn't get any worse when a police car went past with its lights flashing and the siren going and Dog went bonkers.

She was howling just like the siren with her voice going up and down and up and down and I told her to shut up or she'd wake Other Nan, but she wouldn't stop. And so I didn't have a choice, I had to do what I did.

I got the lead that we'd made and I tied it round her neck. Then I pulled her out of the shed and together we ran, the wind pushing us along like leaves, all along Elland Street and round the corner and down Gartside Road and then all the way to 17 Gillespie Street where Paris lives.

Dog was quiet then like she knew this was important and that what happened next could change everything. I felt scared all of a sudden. Before I'd just run without thinking because of having to protect Dog. But now it was really frightening – more frightening than the witch or the flying monkeys – because of it being night out and because the storm was blowing branches off trees and bins all over the road.

But I remembered what Mum had called me – her little soldier. And I told myself that's what I was – a soldier, a brave soldier – and somehow that helped me stop shaking and start thinking slowly and clearly. I knew I couldn't knock on the door because it was thirty-seven minutes past one in the morning according to my glow-in-the-dark Casio watch, but I knew where I could put Dog and I knew where Mrs Potts kept the key – under the gnome having a wee. Anyway, I let us into the garage where it was dry and safe and I sat Dog down in the corner on a lilo which wasn't blown up but was better than the cold concrete. I told her to be quiet and to be patient and that I'd be back in the morning.

Then I texted Paris to tell her what I'd done.

Then I came home.

And I think it will be OK. As long as Dog keeps calm and I keep calm. And as long as Paris gets that text before her mum gets up, because her mum is not highly keen on dogs or any big animals which is why they only have a hamster called Barry. But you can see I didn't have a choice, can't you? If you'd stopped the storm it would have been OK, but you didn't. So I stepped up.

Anyway, I need to try to sleep now because I'm tired and wet and cold and there's a rip in my Batman pyjama bottoms from where I caught them on the door at Paris's.

So, night again.

9 p.m.

When I woke up the storm was gone and the house was silent. I lay in bed and listened, because according to Miss Merriott silence is never really silence when you listen hard enough. She was right because I could hear all sorts of things.

I could hear a sort of hum sound which was Tommo's CD player left on with nothing in it. And I could hear a *drip drip* which is the shower in the bathroom which Dad says he'll fix but probably not until Kingdom Come. But then I could hear another sound. Not in the house this time but outside, from the garden. It was Tommo and he was crying.

And then I remembered.

My hair and pyjamas were still damp and my legs ached as if I had run across the world not just round to Gillespie Street and back. But I didn't care about them, all I cared about was Tommo and Dog, so I pulled on my jumper over my clothes and ran downstairs to get my wellies then I was out the back door as fast as a greyhound.

They were at the shed – Tommo and Johnny and Dad and Other Nan. Dad and Other Nan were trying to tell Tommo to stop crying but he wouldn't stop it and I knew why.

Dad saw me and said, "Sleeping Beauty's up then."

It was supposed to be a joke. And I could have said something back about Dad being the opposite of Sleeping Beauty because his face was all creased and under his eyes there were dark circles like he'd hardly slept in days. But nothing felt funny right then. It all felt grown-up and bad because I had to stop Tommo before he said anything.

"Tommo," I said. But he was too busy pointing at the shed.

Other Nan said, "Why are you all wet?"

I thought quick then and said, "I just had a shower."

"And put your pyjamas back on?" she said.

I said, "I heard Tommo and I was worried." So that bit at least wasn't a lie.

"Lord knows what's got into him," Dad said. "It's just the roof gone." And he pulled off another bit of roof, just like the bit that clattered down the road last night. "Time I took it down anyway, so might as well be now."

Tommo did another wail then and looked at me and I tried to tell him with my telepathic thoughts that Dog was safe but the storm might have messed up the airwaves because he carried on crying.

I looked at Johnny then because I'd tried to think quick but he's older so he's supposed to be wiser, although like Dad says you wouldn't always know it.

"I . . . " he began.

But Other Nan interrupted. For once it was something highly useful. "Don't talk rot," she said to Dad. "You want to be getting some sleep this minute, or you'll only saw your own arm off."

"Thanks for the vote of confidence," he said.

"I'm only trying to be helpful," she said.

Dad was quiet then, which is good because it gave Johnny's brain time to actually come up with something, which was that he would nail some plastic over the roof for now to keep the STUFF dry until MONDAY. And he said "stuff" and "Monday" a bit strange and looked at me strange too, as if what he was actually saying was "and where IS the stuff?"

And I got it. It was a secret code like in World War Two. And I'm good at code, Miss Merriott said so in school. Anyway, I thought maybe I should stop trying to be telepathic and do some code instead so I said, "Dad, can me and Tommo go round to PARIS'S HOUSE?" And I said "Paris's house" loud so that Tommo might understand.

Only he didn't, not yet. But Other Nan said something else useful, which was, "What do you want to go there for?"

Which meant I could say, "Because she's got something SPECIAL to show us, hasn't she, Tommo? I think it might be a new PET."

Tommo stopped sniffing and said, "What happened to Barry?"

I said, "Nothing. But I reckon she might be getting something BIGGER."

"Like a cat?" he said. Which was annoying, because this wasn't supposed to be a guessing game, it was supposed to be code.

"Not a cat," I said. "Even bigger."

In the end, Other Nan guessed. "A dog? Why would Mrs Potts get a dog when she's pregnant? All the germs. And the hair. And what if it tried to savage the baby?"

"Dogs aren't fierce," Tommo said crossly. "Not all of them."

"Not this one," I said. "This DOG is very kind. And also THIN I think. And she has a rare talent for SINGING."

Other Nan said, "Don't be daft. Dogs can't sing."

And I said, "Well this one can. She's SPECIAL."

And then Tommo got it. And he grinned so wide it was like his whole face was cracking open with joy.

"So can we?" I asked.

"Can you what?" asked Dad back.

"Go to Paris's? We could take her the baby clothes." And I pointed at Dog's bed.

"They're filthy," Other Nan said. "And what if

it's a girl? She's not going to want to wear Power Rangers T-shirts."

"She might," Tommo said. "Hester Bankcroft's a girl and she has hair shorter than mine and wears a Spider-Man suit." Other Nan didn't have anything to say to that and nor did Dad. He just said he'd text to check it was OK with Paris's mum. So he did, and it was.

"Just be back for tea," he said.

Other Nan said, "You're too easy on them. It'll come back to bite you."

I looked at Dad and tried to show him in code that we wouldn't ever bite him, and it's like he could read my mind then because he smiled at me and said, "Go on, boys. Before I change my mind."

So me and Tommo did go on, with a bin bag full of baby clothes and him with his face still wet from crying and me with my pyjamas still wet from the storm. We ran down Elland Street, round the corner and along Gartside Road and on to Gillespie Street and Paris's house. Which is when I realised I hadn't even checked my phone to see if Paris knew about Dog yet.

But she did.

She'd got my text in the middle of the night when she'd got up for a wee and she'd checked on Dog then by going through the kitchen door which goes straight into the garage. And she'd given her two cheese slices and a bowl of water and also stroked her and sung her a bit of "Wings", but only a line because she was worried Dog would howl and Nog would wake up because he's living there now and is a surprisingly light sleeper for someone who snores.

Tommo said, "Could we see Dog now, please?" So me and Paris and Tommo and Sonny all trooped down the hall and through the kitchen and out the special door to the garage and there she was, lying on the lilo still fast asleep.

"Dog," Tommo whispered. But she didn't move a muscle except for her ribs which were going up and down and up and down with her breath.

So he tried a bit louder. But she still didn't flicker even an ear.

So I tried. "Dog!" I called. And her head shot up and she bounded over and nuzzled me and Tommo and Paris and even Sonny, who normally she isn't so keen on because he is quite loud and also once tried to ride her for talent practice.

"What did your mum say?" I asked.

Paris said, "She doesn't know. She's usually in bed with a bowl until lunch because of the vomit. And Nog's at work."

"Morning sickness," Tommo said, shaking his head. "The bane of the first trimester."

No one said anything to that because no one understood him. And also we were too busy hugging Dog. Except for Sonny who was investigating the bin bag.

"Why'd you bring Dog's bed?" he asked. "Is she living here now?"

I said no, the clothes were for the baby. Only

Paris said they'd got twenty-four babygrows at TK Maxx plus a Hello Kitty onesie and some formal dresses for parties. I said what if it's a boy but she said they've seen photos and it hasn't got a willy. And she showed us the photo then which just looked like blur to me, but Tommo understood it and pointed out the placenta and the umbilical cord and the no willy.

"It looks like an alien," I said.

Tommo said, "No it doesn't. It's a peanut. It looks like a peanut." And I wanted to give him a hug but I didn't because of Sonny and Paris being there.

Only then he said, "Do you think she'll be OK? Your mum, I mean. When she has her."

"Of course she will," I said quickly. "Because Dad can look after her."

"Why didn't he look after our mum then?" Tommo asked.

I felt sadness in me then, all cold and damp and heavy, like wet clothes. "Because he wasn't trained," I said. "But he is now." And I did give Tommo a squeeze then, but small.

Anyway Paris had other plans for the baby clothes which were to put them on Dog. She found a pale blue cardigan and also a pink tutu which I said was Johnny's from when he wanted to be Angelina Ballerina.

Tommo said, "I thought that was you."

I said, "No. Definitely Johnny." Even though Tommo was right and it was me.

But Paris didn't care whose tutu it was, she just stuck it on Dog.

I said, "I don't think it looks right."

Paris said, "Why not?"

"It's humiliating for her," I said. "A dog in clothes."

"She doesn't care," Paris pointed out. "And anyway, it's her Unique Selling Point. Everyone has to have one to get to the top of the ladder in show business."

I said, "She's a singing dog. What's not unique

about that? Anyway, talent should be about what you do, not what you look like. That's what Miss Merriott said."

Paris said, "But you might as well look good while you're doing it. And besides, it will keep her fresh in the judges' minds."

In the end I had to admit it was certainly unique. Dog didn't seem to mind either way, so we agreed Paris was right and that Dog should wear the cardigan and tutu on stage.

Then we had a brilliant day, God. We had burgers for lunch which Paris made because her mum was still being sick, plus her mum can't even look at meat at the moment, which Paris says is distressing for Nog who doesn't believe in vegetables. After that we did singing with the music turned up so high no one would be able to hear Dog. We did "Wings" five times and "22" four in case we get an encore, but then Mrs Potts banged on the ceiling so we turned it off and decided it was home time.

We wheeled Dog home in the pram and delivered her to the shed which had a new blue plastic roof and even Johnny's old sleeping bag inside for a bed. Other Nan is completely wrong about Johnny – even if he does swear and smoke and stare at boobs he is the opposite of Off The Rails.

Then me and Tommo went inside and Tommo watched *Countdown* with Other Nan and I did some Lego until Dad got up and then we all had tea together, even Johnny. For pudding we were allowed to open an early Easter present from Karol, which was egg boxes with chocolate eggs inside instead of real ones. Johnny ate two and I had one and Tommo had one, and also he offered one to Dad and Other Nan but Other Nan said she valued her teeth, thank you very much, and Dad said, "No, they're for You Boys. I'm all right without."

Then Tommo asked if he could leave the table and Other Nan said no because I was still eating which I was, I was licking out the gooey bit inside of my egg before I started on the chocolate because it makes it last longer. But Dad said yes anyway so off he went. I don't know what he was doing and he wouldn't tell me when I asked but I know he's been on the computer because the last Google search was "how many bees to lift a laptop" which Mythbusters says is a thousand but most other sites say is impossible.

Anyway, the new baby and the eggs got me thinking, God, because it's Good Friday tomorrow and I wondered if that makes you sad because of Jesus dying that day. Also "Good" Friday is a highly unusual name for it when you think about it. I said that to Other Nan because she knows a lot about you, and she said it's called Good because Jesus died to save my sins which is something to be happy about. Dad said Us Boys hadn't done any major sins yet so Jesus had wasted his time on that one, just like Other Nan was wasting hers on all the God stuff. But Other

Nan slammed down her cup of tea and said we were all sinners. I asked what sin she'd done but she said that was between her and you, and then stomped off to get a cloth for the tea. I wish you'd tell me, though. I bet it was coveting her next door neighbour's stuff, for instance Mr and Mrs Norris. Not a bull because they don't have one but maybe their silver Audi A4.

I've done loads of sins. Like I've lied about Dog. And I've stolen money from the swear jar. And I'm always coveting stuff like toys and trainers and even other people's mums.

So I'm sorry.

And I hope I'm worth it. Jesus dying, I mean.

Night.

Friday March 25th

Good Friday

5 p.m.

Dear God,

This isn't a Good Friday at all. In fact, it's the worst Friday ever.

Because Dog is gone.

I don't get it. What's the point of Jesus dying for my sins if I end up getting punished anyway? Or is this another test, like the plague of fleas and the flood and the storm? If it is a test you should come up with another way because like

Miss Merriott says, tests aren't the be all and end all.

Tommo says it's my fault for not checking I'd locked the shed last night but Johnny was supposed to take her for a walk after that so if you think about it it's his fault, only he says it's not because he was tired from all the shed repair and also *Mad Max 3: Beyond the Thunderdome* was on telly so he didn't go out at all, so how can it be his fault and maybe it's actually Tommo's fault.

But like Leia said it doesn't matter whose fault it is, Dog's still missing.

I'd meant to check on her this morning and I was on my way and everything, only then Other Nan shouted at me to come back out of the garden because she needed me for something and I said, "In a minute," only she said, "Not in a minute, *now*."

So I went, thinking whatever it was would only take a minute anyway then I could be back out to see Dog, only the something was that we'd run out of milk and Lord knows where Johnny had got to so could I please go to the corner shop and get a pint of blue or green top, not red because you might as well drink coloured water, which for once I agree with.

So she gave me a pound and I ran out the front door and straight down the road to the corner shop where Mrs Beasley was at the till with Mr Hegarty and Mrs Dullforce who has a moustache, only no one says anything not even Tommo any more. Anyway I was about to grab the blue-top milk out of the fridge when I heard Mr Hegarty saying, "Two of my plant pots were knocked over this morning, and it wasn't the storm this time."

Then Mrs Beasley said, "I heard there was a gang on the loose."

Mr Hegarty said, "But why would they steal my bird food?"

And Mrs Dullforce said, "And your Quavers? Who steals Quavers?"

"Children," said Mrs Beasley. "Small ones who sneak around the back of the aisles."

Mr Hegarty said, "Or midgets."

"Or Muslims," said Mrs Dullforce. "Hiding under them robes. Probably all got crisps on the go under there and all sorts besides."

Then they noticed me standing there and I felt like one of those criminals on telly where they get caught in the shining beam of a policeman's torch.

"It wasn't me," I said quickly. "I don't even like Quavers, I prefer Cheetos."

"Never said it was," said Mrs Beasley. "But your friend Paris Potts was in here yesterday."

"It wasn't her," I said. "She doesn't steal things."

"She does like Quavers, though," said Mrs Beasley.

Which is true, she does, they're her third favourite after Skips and pickled onion Monster Munch but that doesn't make her a thief, which I said.

"What are you up to, anyway?" asked Mrs Beasley then.

"Nothing," I said. "Getting milk."

"Well get it then," said Mrs Beasley.

So I did. I got the milk and I gave her my pound and I got my seventeen pence change with the beady eyes of her and Mrs Dullforce and Mr Hegarty on me the whole time. They watched even as I ran out of the door until it slammed behind me making the cowbells clang.

Then I marched home thinking how I was going to text Paris to tell her what Mrs Beasley was saying now and how she'd change her mind after we won the talent show and were shining stars and rich and famous. But then I suddenly thought who it might have been, which is not midgets or Muslims because that is just Mr Hegarty and Mrs Dullforce being prejudiced like Hitler was against the Jews in World War Two. But someone else who likes bird seed and all flavours of crisp even the ones with no salt on, which Other Nan says are a healthy option and Tommo says are pointless.

Dog.

I ran then, not to the front door but round the back and through the gate and straight to the shed but somehow I already knew what I'd find: the door open and Dog gone.

And she was.

And it felt like the whole whirling world stopped then because if Dog was gone what was the point in anything? I might as well be dead. But I felt bad for thinking that because of Mum so I said sorry to her out loud. And then a strange thing happened which is that I heard her answer me back. Not out loud, because that would be weird, but in my head.

I heard her say, "You can do this. You're incredible, do you know that? The Incredible Billy Wild."

When she said that, I felt the air suck out of me. Because it was sort of like a ghost talking.

But not a scary one, a kind one. And then the air whooshed back in because I knew she believed in me, so I knew I had to do it. I had to find Dog and bring her back.

And I tried. I tried Paris's garage first but she wasn't in there, Nog was cleaning his motorbike.

He said, "If you're after Paris she's down Curl Up and Dye watching her mam get a mani-pedi, whatever one of them is."

I knew what one was because Paris has told me but I didn't say, I just said thanks and closed the door again.

Then I tried the park. I called and called Dog's name and I must've looked mad but I didn't care. She didn't come, though. No one did.

I tried everywhere, God. I tried the school playground and the bus stop and round the back of Abrakebabra where they leave bits of meat in the bins sometimes. Elephant leg, Dad calls it, because that's what it looks like in the window, but he still eats it when he's on a late. But Dog wasn't anywhere.

And then it got worse.

"Oi, you," the voice said.

I looked round quick, thinking maybe someone had found Dog, but when I saw who the voice belonged to it was like my breath got stuck in my body and the world got stuck too for just that second, because right there in front of me was Seamus Patterson with a tan and a hat that said *Lanzarote ain't too grotty*, which is supposed to be funny but I didn't laugh. Because the Pattersons are home.

Then just as quick the world started up again and it was going really fast this time and so were my thoughts, which were what if they'd checked the corrugated sheds and seen that Dog was missing? And what if they were out and about on the hunt for her? And what if they had special dog-detecting equipment? And even though Seamus didn't seem to be on a hunt for Dog, he was mainly eating crisps and watching Fergal do scratch cards, he could just be on a break. And I thought the best thing might be to act normal. To say, "All right, Seamus," or something like that, to try to throw him off the scent. But when I tried a funny noise came out, which just made Seamus laugh at me.

"Billy Weird," he said.

And I know Paris would have said something funny back. Or called him a name. Sassy she calls it. She says it's good for a girl to be sassy. But I'm not a girl and I'm not sassy like her. I'm just Billy. Billy Weird. So instead I did the worst thing possible.

I ran.

I ran hard and fast away, not looking for Dog any more, just trying to get away from Seamus. Even though it made me look suspicious. Even though I could hear him in my head as I ran. "Billy Weird," he was sniggering. "Billy Weird." And I knew he was right. I am weird. I'm not incredible at all. I can't even keep a dog safe.

By the time I got home, I was red from the running and wet from crying, but I wiped it off before Other Nan could see.

"How long does it take to get a pint of milk?" she said when I came in the back door. "Surprised it's not curdled by now."

"They didn't have any at the corner shop," I said. "I had to go to Discount Deals," which is another lie but I didn't even care any more.

"Well where is it?" she said.

And I thought back, and then remembered I'd dropped it when I was running away from Seamus.

"It spilled," I said.

"Oh for heaven's sake, Billy Wild. Useless, you are at times."

"I can get another one," I said, even though I didn't want to.

"No, no. I'll go myself. That way it'll actually get done. You just go upstairs and stay out of trouble."

So I did. I ran upstairs and I told Johnny and Tommo the truth. Not about the milk, but about Dog and about Seamus. I had to, even though I knew Johnny would be worried, which he was, and Tommo would cry, which he did.

"Don't cry," Johnny said. "Remember *Lassie*?"

And I did remember, because it's a film with a dog that finds its way home over a lot of miles so I said, "Yes." And so did Tommo, but he didn't say anything because of the crying. He just nodded.

Johnny said, "Dog's probably gone home. Just like Lassie. She'll have run all the way back to the Pattersons."

And Tommo stopped worrying at that, because he thinks "home" means "safe".

But it doesn't always, does it? Not when it's the Pattersons. Because now they're back, so now Mr Patterson can get his gun and put a bolt through Dog's head and through all the other Good-For-Nowts. When I thought about that I started crying too, only I made Mum say "little soldier" again in my head to make me stop for Tommo's sake.

But not even Mum is helping now.

I just want her back. Dog, I mean. Well, I want Mum back too, but I know that's not statistically possible because of her being dead. But with Dog there's a tiny chance, like smaller than a dot of dirt on an ant but a chance all the same.

I didn't think I'd ever love anything as much as Mum and I never thought I'd be as sad ever in my whole life as I was when Mum died. But I was only four then and I'm ten now, which is more than twice as big, and this sadness feels like it's more than twice as big too. Because I'm sad for all of us and for Dog too.

I know she was never mine in the first place. And I know she's probably gone back where she belongs. But it doesn't make it better.

It makes it much, much worse.

9 p.m.

Another miracle happened, God. Right here in our back garden.

Tommo says it's not a miracle, it's just what Johnny said about Lassie, but I still think that's a miracle.

Because Dog did run home, God. But she ran to ours!

Other Nan was downstairs watching TV, and me and Tommo were lying on our bunk beds trying not to be sad by remembering all the funny things Dog had done – like when she got her nose all orange from Cheetos and when she attacked Tommo's Jabba the Hut and when Paris tied a bow on her tail and she went bonkers and tried to pull it off and ended up going in circles for about ten minutes – when we heard a scuffling noise outside.

We looked at each other and Tommo said, "Are you thinking what I'm thinking?"

Normally I would say no because it's hard to tell

if Tommo is thinking of something obvious or, for instance, how the stripes get into toothpaste. But this time I knew we were both thinking the same thing and that thing was: Dog.

We both rushed to the window and pulled the curtains and there she was, just sitting by the shed door as if nothing had happened.

I could tell Tommo was going to yell at her then so I had to do the shush sign really quickly with my fingers to my lips then I pulled him to follow me to Johnny's room to get his headphones off, and then all three of us went downstairs but slowly and quietly so as not to make Other Nan suspicious. But she was too busy with *Songs of Praise* to notice Us Boys tiptoeing into the kitchen and out the back door.

Once we were out we ran down to the shed and hugged Dog as hard as we could, while she licked our fingers and faces and snuffled in our ears. Then we closed the door behind us and sat down with Dog in the middle and we gave her a good talking to.

Tommo said, "Where did you go then, Dog? Did you go to the museum to see the stuffed walrus?" Because the museum is his favourite local attraction and the walrus is his favourite thing in the museum.

I said, "Don't be daft. Why would she go to a museum? She went on an adventure, didn't you, Dog?"

Johnny said, "I bet she ran for miles."

Tommo said, "Maybe even forty-seven-point-three." Which I know is exactly how far it is to the nearest beach, because he is always saying it to Dad when Dad says it's too far for a day trip.

Which is when I thought, *Maybe she did just run*, because that's what she's born to do, isn't it? It's in her blood. And she hasn't been able to do enough of it what with being shut in the shed.

I said, "It's just until Monday, Dog. Then we'll win Brimley's Got Talent and Dad will love you and he'll love us too and everything will be all right."

Johnny said something then. And it was something I'd been thinking but I had pushed the thought down because it made my stomach swirl too much. That thought was, *What if the Pattersons see?*

Tommo said, "She'll be in disguise in the tutu and the cardigan so they won't recognise her."

Johnny said, "She can't wear a tutu for ever."

Tommo said, "Why not?"

Johnny didn't have an answer for that, and nor did I, so I pretended he hadn't said anything at all. Instead I said, "And then we can take you to the big park, not even in the pram, and you can run all you like."

Tommo said, "But you'll always come home, won't you, Dog?"

"She will," I said.

But I didn't know if that was true, or even which home.

We came in and watched some *Songs of Praise* then and Other Nan said we were Good Boys when we wanted to be. And I said, "I do want to be, I really do."

But it's hard to be good and do the right thing. Sometimes they're not the same. Because even after that I went out to check on Dog twice when Other Nan was having a wee. Tommo's gone back out now to say night-night as well. He'll definitely shut the shed, though. I don't think either of us will ever forget again.

Oh, God, please keep Dog safe. From storms and from the Pattersons and from all the bad things in the world. I'll try to be a Good Boy, I really will, but I wish you'd make it easier to know what good really was.

9.15 p.m.

It turns out Tommo did do a sin after all. Dad got a funny email from someone called HappySally who said she liked his picture because he looked kind and also a bit like an actor called Billy Bob Thornton. Dad said did Us Boys know anything about this, and I said no because I honestly didn't but Tommo went all red. It turns out that the other night he made a profile for Dad on an Internet dating site just like Nice Nan had shown him, and HappySally was Dad's first match.

Tommo said he only did it to get a new mum and it wasn't just because he'd never had one, it was to make Dad happy again. And also because of the lack of Woman's Touch and because he doesn't want to live at Other Nan's.

Other Nan said, "Charming. This is what happens when you let them run riot."

Tommo said, "We're not running at all, we're playing Lego."

And Dad said, "This isn't your business, Gwen," which is Other Nan's actual name.

But Other Nan thought it *was* her business. She said, "This isn't what the boys' mum would have wanted. If you ask me she's looking down now and going spare with worry."

And that's when Dad really lost it. He said,

"No one did ask you. And if she is looking down, which I doubt, because God's a load of old bollocks, the only thing that would be making her spare is you."

Which is when Other Nan stormed upstairs.

No one said a word or moved even a muscle. Not for a whole minute, which I know I counted it in my head. Then Dad looked at Tommo. He said if and when he was ready for a girlfriend we'd be the first to know, but it would more than likely not be until Kingdom Come given he had to be in work in half an hour as it was, and the rest of the time he was asleep or looking after Us Boys, and besides the strike starts in a few days so who wants to go out with an unemployed midwife.

"HappySally might," Tommo said.

Dad said, "I don't want to hear another word, any of you. Tommo, you're banned from the computer for a week."

Tommo said, "Not Google, though."

Dad said, "Even Google."

And then there was another miracle, which is that Tommo didn't cry and that's because Dog had come back so it's two miracles for the price of one when you think about it. Now we only need one more which is to win Brimley's Got Talent on Monday. I know that will be a hard one for you to do because I still don't know all the words, and Tommo and Sonny keep trying to breakdance in the middle. Also every time I think about it, and think about the Pattersons seeing us, I feel a bit sick inside and then I get scared I'll do actual sick on stage, which makes me feel even sicker. But I know it's our Only Hope, God, so I am going to try really really hard. So any help you could offer with that would be excellent.

Night.

Saturday March 26th

10 a.m.

Dear God,

Another miracle has happened and it's one I didn't even ask for and it's that Other Nan has gone home.

She said she had thought long and hard about it and she didn't want to let Us Boys down, but she couldn't stay where she wasn't wanted and so she'd rung Mr Norris from next door and he was picking her up in his silver Audi on his way back from the car wash.

Dad said, "Fine."

And she said, "Fine."

And Tommo said, "Does that mean I can have Coco Pops again?"

And Dad said, "Yes."

Other Nan just tutted at that and said she'd wait in the hallway and could one of us fetch her suitcase so I said I would, only she said, "You can't wait to get rid of me, can you?"

So Dad is right, you cannot win with her.

Anyway Johnny's back in his room and Dad's back in bed and Tommo's on his third bowl of Coco Pops and I'm just waiting for him to finish so we can practise our unique talents with Dog.

4 p.m.

I think you did the wrong miracle. Because if you'd thought about it properly and you had the choice between making Other Nan go home or looking after Dog you'd have picked Dog. That's what I'd have done anyway. But instead Dog got ill.

And I know that's down to Tommo, not you, but you're supposed to have massive powers – bigger ones even than Iron Man or Wolverine – so you could have stopped it if you'd wanted otherwise what's the point?

It was me that found her. I got bored waiting for Tommo so I went out to the shed to give Dog her breakfast and see if she wanted a wee, but when I opened the door I could see she didn't want either and I could see something was really really wrong and I could smell it too.

Dog had been sick. A lot. There were little piles of it all over the sleeping bag like brown soup. And she was shaking – not in the scared way where her legs were all trembling, but bigger this time and sort of jittery, like Tommo gets when it's nearly time to open Christmas presents but not quite.

"What's all that?" said someone behind me and it was Tommo.

"I don't know," I said. "Get Johnny."

But Tommo didn't move. He was too busy

staring at Dog and the sick, plus I thought what if he ran and woke Dad up instead? So in the end I went. I ran back up the path and up the stairs and into Johnny's room and I didn't even knock which usually means you get shouted at or something thrown at you but I didn't care, all I cared about was Dog.

The room smelled of Other Nan and socks and was dark as if it was still night out which is another reason Sonny thinks Johnny might be a vampire. But he's not, he's just a teenager.

I had to shake him to wake him up and I thought he might punch me he looked so angry. But before Johnny could even think about it I said, "It's Dog so you've got to come," and without saying anything back, not even, "It's too early, knobhead," he got out of bed and came down to the shed still in his pants and T-shirt.

He said, "She's eaten something bad."

I said, "She had Quavers yesterday. And bird seed."

Johnny said, "No. This is something else. Poison."

"Like chocolate?" I said, remembering what Paris had said.

Johnny nodded. "Did you give her any?"

"No way," I said.

"Tommo?"

And Tommo went red, so Johnny leaned down and grabbed him by his jumper with both hands and said, "What did you give her?"

"It was only little," Tommo said.

"Little what?" I said.

"Two of Karol's chocolate eggs," he said.

Johnny let go of him and did call him a knobhead then. And Tommo started wailing about how was he to know, and Johnny said he should know because he's King of Bloody Google and what's the point of being the brains of the family if you do something that stupid? So then Tommo called Johnny stupid for getting his neck bitten and Johnny called Tommo a bad swear and

I knew I had to do something to calm them down in case it woke Dad up and also because none of it was helping Dog.

"It'll be OK," I said.

"How?" asked Tommo.

"The vet's," I said. "We've got to take her to the vet's."

"With no one seeing?" Johnny said. "And how are we going to pay for it?"

Tommo said, "I've got four pounds twenty-seven in my R2D2 money box."

Johnny said, "That'll barely pay our bus fare."

But then I remembered about Paris and how she'd got the flea stuff for nothing because her cousin Donna works at Pet Sense which is a pet shop and a vet all in one. And I know Dad says I'm not supposed to actually call people on my mobile unless there's an emergency, but me and Tommo and Johnny decided this was definitely an emergency. So I rang Paris and told her to stop what she was doing and come round now because it was life or death and also to bring the pram. She said, "Awesome," which sounds like she was being rude but it's actually because she is highly keen on drama in everyday situations, like when Sonny nearly cut his finger off with a pair of nail scissors.

Anyway, her and Sonny came round with the pram and between all of us we managed to get Dog in although it wasn't as easy as usual because of her being jumpy and having sick on her. But in the end she was in.

Paris said, "We have to be quick."

I said, "Faster than the speed of light."

Tommo said, "Nothing is faster than the speed of light."

I said, "Shut up and get going."

And he did. And we did.

It was tricky getting on the bus with a pram, especially one with a wriggly dog in it who smells of sick. The driver was not at all keen about it, but Johnny said dogs were allowed and prams were allowed and there was nothing on the sign about not having them both together so he was denying us human rights if he tried to stop us.

The driver said, "Bloody human rights." But in the end he let us on although he did make us park the pram in the special place for buggies. Only even then there was hardly any room and we were squished up with a lady in a hat who kept looking at Dog, and then at us. And I felt my legs go funny because what if she was, say, Mrs Patterson's friend from the bingo and recognised Dog and was going to call her up and they'd call the police to arrest us. But in the end all she said was, "What's that then?"

I said, "A dog."

She said, "Why's it on wheels?"

I said, "She likes it."

She said, "Who can blame her?"

Tommo said, "Who indeed."

That made her laugh and then she gave all of us a mint toffee and Paris and me and Sonny ate ours straight away but Johnny didn't in case it had gelatin in which is meat juice and Tommo didn't because you're not supposed to take sweets off strangers, only by the time we got to the roundabout he'd changed his mind about the hat lady being a stranger and ate it.

We all went quiet then. We were thinking about Dog. I was, anyway. I said, "Will Donna be able to fix her?"

"I doubt it," Paris said. "Donna only does nail-clipping and fancy fur. But the vet will. She's called Pria and she brought Barry back from the dead."

Sonny said, "He was only hibernating because the boiler broke."

Paris said, "Yeah, well she's still a miracle worker."

And the thing is, God, she sort of was.

When we got to Pet Sense the lady on the desk who had eyeshadow in five colours was highly surprised to see Dog in a pram and also highly surprised that we hadn't booked an appointment as they were chock-full all morning. But Paris said, "I know Donna, she's my cousin."

The lady on the desk said, "I don't care if you know the Pope, we're still chock-full."

And Paris was going to say something else and so was Tommo, which was probably something about the Pope because he is dead interested in the Pope, but luckily Johnny was also about to say something, which was, "This is an emergency. Just bloody look!"

And the lady did bloody look, and she didn't even bother to get Donna, she just put us on the list for Pria.

And we had to wait for what felt like for ever but which was probably about twenty minutes and then a lady with dark skin like Manjit Patel and a ring in her nose said, "Billy and Dog. Dog?"

And I said, "Yes. That is actually her name."

So she said, "Come on then, you two." Only it was actually us six, which Pria was surprised about, but no one wanted to stay outside.

And then once we were in the special room, Pria asked us how much chocolate Dog had eaten, and I said, "Two chocolate eggs the size of actual hens' eggs."

And Tommo said, "But the inside isn't chocolate, it's white and yellow fondant that looks like actual yolk but tastes of sugar."

And then Pria gave us some special biscuits for Dog to help with the sickness, and then she said the most amazing three words ever. She said, "She'll be fine."

And I could feel my eyes start to sting and I knew it was tears trying to get out but I didn't want to cry so I rubbed my eyes as if they were itching and just said, "Thanks."

Pria said, "That's all right. Billy, is it?"

I nodded.

Then she told us how the poison in the chocolate makes the dogs all overexcited which is why racers give it to greyhounds sometimes which is against the law, because too much can make them really really ill just like Dog and lots of them die.

I thought I might start to cry again then but Pria interrupted it by saying, "Now, how about I look her over. Make sure nothing else is wrong."

Tommo said, "Nothing else *is* wrong. We love her, you know."

Pria said, "I know you love her. But you need more than love to look after a dog. It's a *big* responsibility, especially a dog like a greyhound, and some people find they can't cope."

Johnny said, "We *can* cope."

Pria said, "I'm not saying you can't. But shall we just check she's OK?"

Johnny shrugged which meant "whatever" which meant yes. So Pria checked.

There was some other stuff wrong after all. Like the fleas which is what had made her chew her fur off and also she needed her nails cutting.

I said, "But . . . "

Only I couldn't finish my sentence, which was

that we don't have enough money, because what if Pria asked why not, and then I'd have to tell her about Dad and Mum and the strike, and I know Miss Merriott says it's good to talk but I'm not sure she meant the vet. Pria looked at me then, and it was like she didn't even need me to say the words because she was looking inside my head and could see the thoughts all just hanging in there, because the next thing she said was, "It's all right, Billy. It's on the house." Which means free.

Johnny asked how come and she said they have clinics for people in certain circumstances and normally they're on a Tuesday night but she was doing a special one that very morning so weren't we lucky. I said we were, and Paris agreed, although Tommo said there was nothing lucky about our circumstances. That made Pria laugh and when she did it made my heart lift again, and a seed of thought got planted in my head which was, *Maybe we could ask her to be our new mum.* Only when it was time to go I couldn't get the words to come out of my mouth, and Johnny said to get a move on because we'd got no money for the fare back and it was a long walk, so I swallowed them down instead.

Pria said we had to promise to feed Dog properly and walk her twice a day once she was recovered and we all promised, and when we got back we gave her some food and water and cleared up the sick, but she just lay on her sleeping bag looking at me with big tired eyes and I felt happysad. Happy because she was alive, but sad that she nearly died and that's because of us.

Maybe Pria's right. Maybe we can't cope. Because all sorts of stuff has gone wrong with Dog and it's mainly mine and Tommo's fault. Maybe Other Nan's right about Dad not coping too – with Us Boys, I mean.

Tommo says now that Other Nan is out of the picture it's next stop social services, he's seen it on *The Dumping Ground* and we'll have to go and live in a massive house with rude girls and Johnny will definitely end up Off The Rails. Johnny said no he wouldn't and that no one's going into care, so to stop being a moron. Only Tommo said, "I've seen it. On TV." Which is his answer to everything. But the thing is the TV is often right, for instance about it being impossible to lick your own elbow, so perhaps Other Nan going this morning wasn't a miracle after all.

And Pet Sense was full of not-miracles. Like there was a cat who had a cancer on its neck as big as a tangerine and the owner let me stroke it (the cat, not the tangerine cancer) but then Pria called her in and when the owner came out her eyes were all red and the cat wasn't with her any more and we knew she'd been put down.

I've seen Dad sometimes with red eyes and even though he says, "Nothing's up, Billy boy," when I ask him, I can tell something is and it's that a baby has died.

Big Sue says he's not supposed to get attached otherwise he'll be weeping left, right and centre, but Karol says it's hard not to when you've known the mums so long. I asked, "Why do you do it then?" And Karol said because of the other tears – the good ones when babies are born healthy and everyone cries with happiness.

That's what must have happened to me at the vet's today. All the fat happiness that Dog was alive must have pushed some tears out.

But other tears are coming now, God. Sadness ones. For the cat with the tangerine cancer and for what nearly happened with Dog and for Other Nan going home when she's not actually evil like, say, Hitler, she just moans a lot. And for all the bad things that happen in the world.

And because I'm not sure you're even real at all, God.

Sunday March 27th

Easter Sunday

7 p.m.

Dear God,

I'm sorry for saying what I said last night. I just wish I knew for sure if you were actually there or not, or how much you're listening or even watching me and Tommo and Johnny and Dog. Because sometimes I think maybe you're not all that interested in, say, what I had for breakfast or even cats with tangerine tumours because you've already seen it happen. And sometimes I wonder if maybe you actually speak French or Polish or Japanese and I may as well be talking to myself because I am utterly a mystery to you.

At least when I talk to Dog I can tell she's listening.

After breakfast, which was two bowls of cornflakes not Coco Pops because Tommo said what if Dog swallowed an atom of chocolate off us and was ill again, we went back to the shed and I told Dog all about what happened yesterday in case she was so ill she had forgotten. Dog seemed to understand how sad we'd been because when I said about all the crying she scrabbled right into my lap and put her head on my shoulder with a big sigh. It is quite hard having a greyhound in your lap, God, because they are mostly leg and there are four of them, and as soon as they get one in, another one pops out. But I didn't mind, I stayed like that for ages, with legs everywhere and her warm tummy on my thighs, and her breath in my ear. And I told her about what was going to happen tomorrow as well, and reminded her what she had to do and why. "You're going to sing," I said. "And I'm going to be incredible."

"Me too," said Tommo. And even though it's supposed to be The Incredible Billy Wild, not The Incredible Tommo Wild, I didn't say anything because I know it's unfair that I don't have a mum any more, but he never had one in the first place.

Anyway, then Tommo said, "Crunch time tomorrow." And did the "der-der-DER" noise which you get in cartoons when something bad is about to happen, which wasn't helpful at all which I was about to point out, only then Dad shouted out the back door to get back in or our food would get cold, so we did.

And it was like Dad was a new person, because he'd had a shave and was wearing normal clothes i.e. not hospital clothes, and he'd made special Easter lunch i.e. a choice of roast chicken or fake vegetarian chicken, with two different kinds of potatoes i.e. mashed and roasted, which is

Tommo's second favourite lunch after spaghetti bolognese and my first favourite.

Only today I wasn't really hungry.

Dad said, "You'd better not be going down with something, Billy Boy."

I said, "I'm not."

Tommo said, "He's just nervous."

I said, "Am not," and kicked him under the table.

He said, "Are so," and tried to kick me back but his legs are too short and he missed and got Johnny instead who kicked him back only harder, which made Tommo cry.

Dad said, "Flaming hell. I don't know why I bother sometimes. I might as well just stay at work and have Big Sue in one ear and Little Sue in the other."

So I said, "Sorry, Dad."

And Tommo said, "Sorry, Dad."

Johnny didn't say anything, but he didn't moan either and he ate four carrots which Tommo said was progress.

"Why are you nervous, Billy?" Dad asked then.

I said, "I don't know." Which is a lie but I've told so many I don't think one more matters really.

Dad sighed and said, "Look, I'm sorry. I know it's been tricky this holiday. And I can't promise it'll get any easier either with the strikes starting Tuesday. But I'm off tomorrow so we can do something together."

Tommo said, "Like we could all go to Brimley's Got Talent."

Dad said, "I was thinking more we could make a start on the shed, then have a bonfire."

The "No!" came out of my mouth before I could think quick enough to stop it.

"Why not?" Dad said. "You and Tommo love a bonfire. Everyone loves a bonfire."

Which is true because they're fierce exciting and you get to burn all sorts of stuff to see what colour it turns the flames, for instance magazines and bits of cardboard and once some old socks which made it go blue which was highly excellent. But

I couldn't love this bonfire so I looked at Johnny then for help and even though he had a mouthful of mash he managed to say, "Environment," which made some potato fly out on to the table.

Dad said, "It's like you were raised by wolves. Swallow your food before you say anything."

So Johnny swallowed and said it again. "Bad for the environment, bonfires. Leia says."

Only Dad didn't want to know what Leia says because Leia says a lot of things and they are usually about how Dad is wrong.

"Please can we go," I said then. "To the show, I mean. We can do the shed after. And other stuff. Like clean the windows, say. Or tidy our rooms."

Dad said, "Blimey, you really are going down with something."

I said, "I'm not. I just really want to go to the talent show. We all do."

And Tommo and even Johnny nodded at that.

And then Dad put down his knife and fork, like

he was about to say something important. And he was.

"Fine," he said. "But if all it is is Morris dancing and Mrs Johnson reading her poetry, I'll be out of there faster than you can say 'shenanigans'."

Tommo said shenanigans then, just to himself, to test it out, and it's actually quite fast. But I didn't care, because Dad's coming, and that's part one of the plan done.

Only now I'm even more worried, because now it's just down to us, and down to me to be incredible. And I'm not sure I am, God. I'm really not.

I texted Paris and she said I just need to have faith, because believing in yourself is half the battle. And also to have a light breakfast with no dairy products, for instance yoghurt, because that can clog the vocal chords.

But I'm not sure Paris is right. About the yoghurt or the faith. What if we get up on stage and everyone just laughs? Then I won't be The

Incredible Billy Wild at all. I'll just be Billy Weird with a dog in a cardigan. And we won't get famous and have loads of money so Dad won't be able to stop work and love Us Boys instead. And, worse, even if Dad's heart does melt the Pattersons might see us so Dog will have to go back after all and live with the other poor dogs who smell like Dead Grandpa and howl out their sadness.

I told Dog about it – not about her going home, but about being scared – and she licked my hand which might have been because it had some dried chicken gravy on it or might have been a sign that she understood. It'd be nice if you could send me a sign like that too.

I'm not saying I want you to lick my hand because that would be like the biggest miracle ever and also highly unusual. But if you could just show me you were even listening that would be nice.

Night.

Monday March 28th

Easter Monday
1 p.m.

Dear God,

When I woke up, I could tell something wasn't right because normally when Dad is off on a bank holiday he's in the kitchen cooking bacon and playing music from the olden days. Only today there was no music and no meaty smell at all and in fact no Dad. Instead there were three bowls set out on the kitchen table and a box of Rice Krispies, and a note that said:

Change of plan, sorry boys. Gone into work. Karol and me'll be back after tea for some shed bashing, though!

Love Dad.

PS No more than a spoon of sugar each.

PPS Get Johnny up.

My first thought was to cry, because right there in that note was the end of all our plans and hard work. All the bother we'd got into had been for nothing, because now Dad wasn't coming because he'd gone back to the hospital because he'd made his choice and work was all that mattered, not Us Boys.

Then I thought something else, which was that I hadn't actually told him I was in the show. And so maybe if he knew that, and how badly I wanted him to come, then he'd change his mind.

And my third thought was, *I'm going to change his mind.*

I didn't get Johnny up. I didn't even get

Tommo. I did it on my own. I got dressed and I got my coat and my shoes on and I gave Dog her breakfast and told her I'd be back soon. And she gave me a snuffle in my ear, which I think meant "I know, Billy."

And then I took some money out of the swear jar, went to the bus stop, and got on the number 13 to the hospital.

The hospital smells of disinfectant and dinner. Most people say they don't like hospitals because of the smell and also all the death and illness, but I don't mind them because Dad's ward isn't about death it's about life. Everyone loves a baby, that's what he says.

You're supposed to stop at reception when you get there, to ask directions, but I knew exactly where to go because I've been loads. So I just walked straight to the lifts and got in one with a man wearing a yellow jumper, which Paris would say was a bold fashion choice, but I didn't say anything. I just pressed the number 3 and waited for the doors to close and the lift to judder and then go up.

The man said something, though. "You visiting too?" he asked.

"Yes," I said.

"My wife's in," he said. "Ten pounds two it was. It's our first."

I nodded. "My dad's in," I said. "It's approximately his five thousandth."

The man didn't say anything after that.

Big Sue was on reception. She looked about as happy to see me as she usually is to see Dad.

"Billy Wild," she said. "What are you doing here?"

"I need to speak to my dad," I said.

"Not now you don't," she said, looking at a chart. "He's in a breach in room 4." That's a baby being born bottom-first, which is difficult, but not impossible, Dad says.

So I said I'd wait, but I didn't. As soon as she

was looking at her charts again I turned around and walked towards the delivery area, and when the man from the lift got buzzed in I just walked in behind him like I was his son.

Room 4 was on the left and even though the door was shut I could hear sounds from behind it. I could hear a mooing noise, which I knew was the mum having the baby, then I heard a man saying, "Oh god, is she OK?" which I knew was the dad. Then I heard another voice, and it said, "She's going to be fine. She's doing brilliantly. You hear that, Kylie? You're going great guns."

And that was my dad. I felt proud then, because he was being kind and helpful and also it is not an easy job looking at ladies' vaginas all day, or getting shouted at by the ladies because the vaginas are hurting. But I also felt sad that he would rather do that than come to the talent show with Us Boys.

So I knocked on the door.

Karol opened it and when he saw it was me his

eyes went all goggly. "Danny," he said. "It's for you."

And then Dad came out in his scrubs, which are basically a green shirt and trousers, with a plastic apron over the top for all the blood and poo. And he looked at me, and I wished then that his face would turn into a massive smile, and he'd say, "Billy. I forgot! I'm coming this minute." But instead it was like he'd seen a zombie, because his forehead creased and his mouth went open but no sound came out. Until it did. And the sound wasn't a good one.

He hissed, "Jesus, Billy." Then he looked behind him and pulled the door to, and said it again only louder this time. "Jesus, Billy," he said. "How did you even get here?" And I was about to say, "By number 13 bus," but Dad said, "No, don't even tell me. I don't want to know. But I do want to know what the hell you think you're doing? Karol and me, we're in the middle of a delivery here."

"I'm sorry," I said.

"Did you not get my note?" he asked.

"Yes," I said. "But I think you might have forgotten about the talent show."

Dad's forehead got even more creased then. "Are you joking?" he asked.

I shook my head.

Dad closed his eyes then, like he was trying to make everything better. But when he opened them it hadn't worked.

"Listen. It's a talent show, and I know it would've been a laugh, but this came up and I had to take it."

"But you don't understand—" I began, but Dad interrupted.

"No *you* don't understand," he said. "We need the money. You can still go and watch, though, Johnny'll take you."

"But that won't work," I said.

"What won't work?"

And I could've told him then, that we weren't just watching, we were actually in it, me and

Tommo. But the door open, and Karol said, "Danny? You're needed."

So I just said, "Nothing."

Which was the wrong thing to say.

"Nothing?" Dad said. "Really? Nothing? You've come all this way, and dragged me out of a breach, for nothing?"

I shrugged.

"Go home," he said. "Go home now, and I will deal with you later." And his face was tight and his eyes were tired and I knew that I had better shut up and do what he said. So I did. I walked back out the buzzy doors and past Big Sue and I didn't stop when she called my name after me I just went straight down the stairs and out and to the bus stop, and that's when I started crying.

When I got back Tommo was in the shed with Dog talking to her about *Sherlock*. Dog looked a bit confused, and I'm not surprised, because *Sherlock* can be quite confusing. But when I came in she stood up and pushed her face into my hand. And I took a biscuit off the shelf and gave it to her and she sat down happily, crunching her treat.

"Where've you been?" Tommo said. "Have you been crying? Why're you crying?"

"Hospital," I said. "And no. Just that there's an emergency."

Tommo said, "Is it octuplets?" Because he is highly keen on octuplets or any multiple births.

I said, "No. It's that Dad won't come to the talent show, so we have to think of a Plan B."

Tommo looked disappointed at that but he did at least have an answer, and that was, "We should ask Johnny."

And so we did.

We both went to get Johnny up because it's easier as a two-man job i.e. one to pull the duvet off and one to hand him a Mars bar so he doesn't hit you.

He said, "You're such a pair of knobs."

Tommo said, "Fifty pence but I will let you off because this is an emergency."

Johnny pulled the duvet back over him and said, "Like what?"

I pulled it off again and said, "Like Dad's gone to work."

Tommo added, "So he won't be coming to the talent show."

Johnny said, "How do you know?"

Tommo said, "Because he left a note."

And I said, "Also I went to ask him to change his mind and he said no."

Which is when Johnny said a bad swear.

I said, "I'll give you my pudding for a whole week if you help us."

"Me too," said Tommo. "Except if it's jam roll."

Johnny made an angry noise then like he was going to kill one of us so we stepped away from the bed, but it was actually just him preparing to get up which is quite a difficult task for him even not being a vampire.

"Fine," he said.

"Really?" Tommo asked.

"Really," Johnny said. "OK. This is what we'll do. One, we eat lunch. Two, you text Paris to meet us here with the pram ay-sap."

I said, "What's ay-sap?"

He said, "A.S.A.P? As soon as possible? Duh."

I said, "No need to duh me."

He said, "Well stop interrupting then."

I said, "I have."

He said, "Omigod, just be quiet, will you? Three, you take Dog to the talent show. And four, I go to the hospital to get Dad."

"But he didn't listen to Billy," Tommo said. "Why will he listen to you?"

Johnny sighed. "If I tell him you've done something really stupid he'll have to come," he said.

"Like what?" I asked.

"Like the truth," he said. "Like breaking the law."

I felt the humpback bridge feeling then, like my insides had flipped over. But I knew beggars can't be choosers so telling the truth it was. "And then what?" I said.

Johnny said, "Well that bit's up to you, isn't it? You sing, I suppose."

I said, "What if it doesn't work?"

Johnny said, "God, I don't know. This was your stupid idea. I'm only trying to help."

Tommo said, "We could mesmerise everyone and be the First Human Boys to hypnotise Brimley."

Johnny said, "Jesus, Tommo. You're so weird you make Billy look normal."

Tommo said, "You're quite blasphemous today."

Johnny said, "It can't be blasphemy if I don't believe in it. If there was a God, do you think we'd be trying to come up with a plan right now?"

Which even Tommo had to admit was a bit suspicious.

I didn't say anything, though, God. Because I

was trying to have faith. So hard that I didn't hear what Johnny said so he had to repeat it.

"I said, you'd better get a bend on and text Paris then," he said.

So I did.

And now we're just waiting.

For Paris to get here with Sonny and the pram.

For Dad to be persuaded to come to the village hall.

For the Pattersons not to see us.

And for Dog to sing and melt hearts and me to be The Incredible Billy Wild.

Like Tommo said, it's Crunch Time. And I am trying to be brave, be a little soldier, but Mum seems to have lost her voice too, God. So it looks like it's just down to me now. And I'm not sure I can do it on my own.

I'm not sure at all.

7 p.m.

I'm scared of a lot of things. For instance:

- Aliens taking over the Earth by disguising themselves as humans.
- A rat swimming up through the sewer and into our toilet just as I sit down for a poo.
- Calling Miss Merriott "Dad" by mistake in class.
- Spelling tests.
- Seamus Patterson.

But I have never been as scared of anything in my life as I was taking Dog to Brimley Village Hall in a pram pushed by Paris Potts.

We'd draped one of our old net curtains over the hood so no one could see in and it's not like Dog was keen to make a noise anyway, but there was still danger everywhere today because all the village was out and about and being beady.

The first people we bumped into were Mr and Mrs Beasley who had left Bald Alan in charge of the shop just so they could come to the show, which if you knew Bald Alan you'd know how highly unusual that was.

"What are you lot up to?" Mrs Beasley asked.

"Practising," said Paris. "For when the baby comes."

Mrs Beasley went bright red when she said that. "How old are you?" she said.

"Ten and a half," said Paris. "But my mum's thirty-one and a quarter and Nog's thirty-four and nearly a month, which is actually above average for a first-time parent."

"How old are you?" Tommo asked Mrs Beasley.

Mrs Beasley didn't like that. "That's none of your beeswax," she said and stomped off with Mr Beasley sort of scuttling behind.

"He is a downtrodden man," Tommo said, because that's what Dad says. "We should pity him."

So we did pity him, all the way along Gartside Road and on to the High Street which is where I stopped pitying anyone except me because right there kicking an empty Tango can against the bus stop were Seamus Patterson and his best mate Mason Pedley. Seamus was wearing the Lanzarote cap again and Mason was wearing his City kit and I could feel my Rice Krispies milk going sour in my stomach.

"This is a mental idea," I said. "Let's go back."

"We can't," said Paris. "Otherwise your dad'll be even crosser if he's dragged out of the hospital and you're not even on stage."

"S'pose," I said.

"And there's no point going back to the shed," she added.

"Its hours are numbered," said Tommo.

"The shed's dead," said Sonny. And then him and Tommo started chanting "the shed's dead" which is when Seamus and Mason saw us.

Seamus said, "It's Billy Weird."

And Mason said, "And his girlfriend," and then laughed with a "hunh-hunh-hunh" sound like a monkey.

I wanted to say, "I'm not weird, and she's not my girlfriend," but Paris got in first. "You're the weird one, Seamus Patterson," she said. "Everyone thinks so. Especially Lacey Prendergast," who Seamus likes only he pretends not to according to Paris.

Mason did his monkey laugh at that but Seamus told him to shut up and then he told us to shut up and then he just walked off with Mason kicking the can after him.

But that didn't make me feel any better. "I bet they're going to the show," I said.

"So what if they are?" said Paris. "Who cares what they think?"

"Not me," said Sonny.

"Not me," said Tommo.

"Er, yes we do?" I said. "Because when Seamus spots Dog he'll call his dad and then they'll take her back and everything will have been for nothing."

Paris said, "You're catastrophising," which is

when you imagine the worst thing happening and then don't do something in case it happens. Tommo said there were loads of worse things that could happen, for example a boy-eating dinosaur could come round the corner right now, or possibly Other Nan. But Paris said he wasn't helping and we should all just get a move on or we'd be late and then what was the point and we might as well just walk into the police station and be done with it.

I said that was catastrophising and Tommo said me saying that was catastrophising and Sonny said he was catastrophising right now and pretended to die. But then Dog did a fart and we realised maybe we should get on.

As we started walking Tommo said, "Maybe she could fart 'Wings' instead?"

I said, "Maybe you could fart 'Wings'."

Sonny said, "Maybe we could all fart 'Wings'."

Paris said, "Girls don't fart."

Which isn't actually true because I've heard Other

Nan do it, but I didn't say anything because I didn't want to upset Paris and also because by then we were at Brimley Village Hall. I'd sort of expected it to have flags out, or balloons, or even just the tinsel left over from Christmas but there was just a poster with the word "TODAY!" written across it. Next to that was Mrs Osterley who runs Cubs, holding a money bag and a roll of raffle tickets.

She said, "That'll be a pound each, please."

Paris said, "We're not watching, we're being talented."

Mrs Osterley did not look entirely convinced but she checked her list and saw that we *were* actually being talented and said we should go round the back of the hall to wait in the dressing room i.e. the toddler group play area. We were just about to go when she said, "Where do you think you're going with that pram?"

Paris said, "Round the back like you said."

Mrs Osterley looked annoyed and said, "What's in the pram?"

Paris said, "It's our props."

Mrs Osterley said, "It's a fire hazard is what it is, you'll have to leave it next to the bike rack and fetch what you want out of it when it's your turn."

Paris said, "What if it had a real baby in it?"

Mrs Osterley said, "Does it?"

Paris said, "No."

Mrs Osterley said, "So stop arguing and get round the back."

When we got round the back we parked the pram, and I lifted the blanket up a bit so we could talk to Dog.

"It's nearly time," I said.

And Paris said, "Don't worry. We're going to be brilliant."

"Are we?" I asked.

Then Paris shushed me and dropped the blanket and said, "You have to talk the talk and walk the walk no matter how bad you're feeling."

"Oh," I said.

"How bad do you feel?" asked Tommo. "On a scale of one to ten."

"Which is which?" I asked.

"Ten is brilliant and one is being eaten by zombies."

"Two," I said.

Tommo shook his head and Paris rolled her eyes, then lifted up the blanket again. "Brilliant, do you hear me?" she said.

But Dog looked at her like she didn't hear her. So I said it too. "We're going to be awesome," I said.

"And also excellent," said Tommo.

"And outstanding!" said Sonny.

Dog sighed and lay down then.

"And incredible," I said, only quieter this time, just to Dog. "I'm going to be incredible. The Incredible Billy Wild!"

"Come on," said Paris. "Let's check out the competition."

So we did. Tommo and Sonny sat with the pram at the bike rack and me and Paris went backstage.

Almost everyone was in a mad costume e.g. Mr Baxter from the garage in a top hat and Mrs Johnson who is our dinner lady in tap shoes and a very tight dress the colour of strawberry Angel Delight.

Paris said, "That is an ill-advised look, given her body shape, which is a definite apple. Also it doesn't tone with her skin."

Normally I would be quite interested in this, but right then all I could think was, *Please let Dad show up* and *Please* don't *let the Pattersons show up.* I peered behind the curtain to see and all the rows of metal seats were getting full and there were people crowding behind as well. I peered really hard but I couldn't see the Pattersons, or Johnny and Dad.

"What if he doesn't come?" I said. "Dad, I mean."

"Course he will," said Paris. "He's your dad."

"So where's yours?" I asked.

"Telford," she said. "But Nog's here."

And I looked and he was there sitting with Mrs Potts right in the front row behind the judges, who were the mayor, and Mrs Bottomley who runs the church choir, and our headmaster Mr Nesbit. And there were loads of other people too – I could see Miss Merriott from school, and Mr and Mrs Beasley, and Leia. I tried to count the whole audience but after seventy-something I lost my place.

"I don't think I can do it," I said.

"Count?" Paris asked.

"No, sing."

"Yes you can," Paris said. "You can definitely do it, and so can the rest of us and so can Dog and all."

"How do *you* know?" I said.

Paris looked at me as if I was bonkers. "Because I've got faith," she said.

"In who?" I asked.

"In you."

And that was the last thing either of us said

because then Mrs Osterley turned the lights out and Mr Eggs who is the caretaker at school and who was in charge of the CD player played the theme from James Bond, which meant the show was about to begin. So we walked the walk back through the toddler room and sat down on the wall outside with Tommo and Sonny and a pram full of Dog.

We didn't see any of the other acts, but we could tell how well they did by the clapping. Mrs Johnson got medium claps and Mr Baxter got loads, but most claps went to the Norton twins who are in Tommo's year and who are both highly promising gymnasts according to Tommo's teacher and highly annoying according to Tommo.

Then it was our turn.

Mrs Osterley stuck her head out the back door and said, "Chop chop, you lot." So we did. We stood up and then we lifted the blanket and took Dog out and put her on the ground. Her cardigan was half off and her tutu was very creased but she still looked smart and she looked pleased to be out as well.

"It's time," I said to her and I stroked her head.

"Crunch time!" said Tommo.

"Shut up," I said and I held Dog's ears down so she couldn't hear.

"No, you shut up," said Tommo.

"You'd all better shut up," said Mrs Osterley. She was looking at Dog funny, and I thought she might stop us, but she said, "I suppose you'd better get that thing inside then. Sharpish."

As we went through the dressing room, one of the Norton twins – I don't know which as they are completely identical – said, "I didn't know you had a dog, Tommo Wild."

Tommo said, "I'm a mystery, me."

The other one said, "Why's it wearing a tutu?"

Tommo said, "It's a she, not an it, and she's also a mystery."

The first one said, "She smells."

Sonny said, "You smell."

Then Mrs Osterley said, "No one smells, now will you get on stage before I disqualify you and get Mrs Stephenson on with her hand bells."

So we did.

We walked out on to the stage and I was looking really hard again, checking faces to see if one of them was Dad. But before I could do the third row, Mrs Osterley came out and looked at her list and said, "And now it's Paris and Sonny Potts and Billy and Tommo Wild with their band ... Dogstar. Is that right?" And I nodded and she disappeared off again and then it was just us and Dog, with the lights shining down and the faces of the audience staring up. It was weird that moment. Like I wanted it to end because I felt so sick, but also last for ever because it was so amazing.

And I realised I was holding my breath and let out a massive burst of air just as someone shouted, "Billy? Jesus, Billy, what the flaming hell have you done this time?"

And I looked, and there, right at the very back, was Johnny, with a red face, and next to him, still in his green scrubs, was Dad.

"See I told you," said Paris. "I said he'd show up."

And I felt something in me soar up then, like a big burst of butterflies, or a note even, ready to come out, ready to sing.

"Billy?" Dad said my name again. But I didn't answer, because I was ready, more ready than I'd ever been. So I nodded at Tommo who nodded at Sonny who nodded at Paris who nodded at Mr Eggs who pressed play on our backing track.

And after the opening notes played, we took deep breaths, and we started to sing.

Me and Paris and Sonny and Tommo. All of us.

All except Dog.

I looked at Paris in panic but she just nodded at me to keep going so I did. But we got to the second chorus and Dad was pushing his way through the crowd trying to get to the stage, and Dog was still just standing there staring at the audience with her legs shivering and I could feel mine doing the same, but I knew I had to do something, I had to walk the walk for her before Dad stopped me, so I went and I pressed stop on the CD player.

Mr Eggs said, "You're not authorised to touch the equipment."

And Paris said, "Are you going mad, Billy?"

But instead of saying "no" like I normally would I said "maybe". And then I took Dog's lead and I led her right to the front of the stage and made her turn around so she was just looking at me. Then I leaned down. "We can do this," I said. "Me and you, together. I really believe it. I have faith. Do you understand?"

And Dog snuffled my ear, and licked it. And I knew she did.

Then I stood up again and took a massive breath. And I started to sing. Just me on my own. And not "Wings" this time.

Instead I started singing "Danny Boy". That song Mum used to sing, do you remember? And me too sometimes, on my own, and quiet.

Only this time I sang it loud. And I sang it right at Dad.

"Oh Danny Boy, the pipes, the pipes are calling," I sang.

Dog didn't join in but I kept on anyway.

"From glen to glen," I sang. "Across the mountainside."

And I took another breath and was about to sing the next line when something incredible happened. Dad stopped pushing, and he started singing. Right at me. And right at Dog.

I hadn't heard him sing for years I realised then, so it was a surprise. His voice was deeper than mine, and different to Mum's, but he knew all the words, just like she did. "The summer's gone, and all the flowers are dying," he sang.

Then together we sang the next line, "Tis you, tis you must go and I must bide."

I was so surprised I stopped then, but Dad carried on and nodded at me to keep going like Paris had done, so I started again. And so did Tommo and Paris and Sonny.

And then other people started to join in. Karol stood up first and even though he didn't know the words he sort of "la"ed along.

And then Mrs Potts and Nog stood up and sang.

And then Mr Beasley stood up. Mrs Beasley tried to pull him back down by his raincoat but he shook her off and started singing.

Until almost everyone in the hall was singing "Danny Boy" at the tops of their voices.

All apart from Dog.

"Come on, girl," I said. "You can do it, go on."

And then it was like magic. Because she looked at me, then back out at the audience, then she sat down on the floor and put her head back and howled.

And then everyone went silent again, and it was just Dog and me and Dad.

And we sang and we sang and we sang, until the very last verse, until the line about sleeping in peace, which is when someone else piped up, and it wasn't the right words, it was something else entirely.

"Oi. That's not your dog!"

I looked, and right there, next to the toilet sign, stood Seamus Patterson, and next to him on either side were all the other Pattersons.

And I knew then that even if Dad did love Dog they'd still take her back. Back to all the other Good-For-Nowts, and to the bolt. And I knew then I couldn't stay. Not in the hall, not with everyone staring and frowning – the Pattersons, Dad, Nog, Mrs Beasley – all of them. I had to get out.

And so did Dog.

I knew if I ran right away, though, they'd catch me, so I thought hard, God. Harder than I'd thought in my whole life. Then I turned round and said, "Come on, girl." And I didn't listen to the audience murmuring or wondering what the hell I thought I was playing at. And I didn't listen to Dad shouting at me to stop. I just walked the walk all the way past Tommo and Sonny and Paris, all the way behind the curtain, all the way through the toddler room, where the Norton twins were still doing the splits, and out the back door.

Then I said it.

"Run," I yelled. Then, my heart bang-banging already in my chest, I leaped towards the gap in the hedge, and set off for the park.

Dog didn't need telling twice. She flew behind me. And this time she didn't bound away and come back again, she stayed right at my side. It's like she knew this wasn't a game. This was life or death. For real.

We ran right across the park and then out on to Gartside Road, and all the while I could hear voices shouting in the background, "Billy! Come back, Billy."

But I didn't come back, I carried straight on.

Past Mrs Beasley's shop, past our road and off towards the edge of the village.

I didn't know where I was going when I left the village hall, but as soon as I was out it seemed like it was the only answer. Maybe I couldn't keep Dog. But I could do something else. And it was like you'd given me a sign, God, because it was right there in the front of my brain, and what it was saying was, "Go to the farm, Billy. Go to the Pattersons' farm, and set all the dogs free."

So I did. I ran and ran all the way to the lane where Little Sue had dropped us off, but I didn't stop, and nor did Dog this time. We ran all the way up, until we could see the corrugated sheds, and then we slowed down, and then we stopped just outside the yard.

I could smell it from outside – the sadness, the Dead Grandpa smell, only worse, because there was poo mixed in and all. It smelled of meanness and cruelty and hurt. And I knew I was doing the right thing. I was giving them a chance.

Then I smelled something else too, or maybe I imagined that part, because when I say it you'll probably think I'm bonkers. Because it was like a seed of faith had finally started to grow inside me and a flower had opened its petals and the scent it gave off was hope.

And then it happened. Without me even thinking about it. My feet started walking towards the sheds, and my arms went up and I pulled back the lock and I opened the door. And then I went up to one of the metal cages inside, and I pulled back the lock on that too.

"There you go," I said to the dogs inside. "You're free."

Then I opened another cage, and another and another, until all the cages in that shed were open, then I did the other two sheds as well until I'd opened maybe a hundred cages. At first the dogs didn't seem to understand at all. They sort of milled around the yard smelling things and then weeing on them. Then I realised – they didn't know what freedom was. They'd not run in the park like Dog, with the wind in their fur and their tails whipping. They'd only been at a track, following a fake rabbit on a trolley.

I needed to explain it. Or rather, we did. Me and Dog.

She'd been waiting in the yard until then, stood exactly where I left her, just watching all the other dogs like they were mad. But now she looked at me, and it was like she could see inside my head and read my thought, my telepathic thought. And the thought was, *Let's show them.*

And we ran then, out the yard. Not fast yet, because the dogs were still smelling and weeing and some of them were trying to eat a piece of wood. But then one of them saw us and started to follow. And as soon as one dog was running, another one started, then another. And then all the dogs were trotting down the lane behind me and Dog, and then around me and Dog, because now they'd got a taste of it, they wanted to speed up.

And then all the dogs weren't just trotting, they were sprinting past, yelping and bounding like mad March hares.

I stopped then, and so Dog did too. And we just stood and watched for a second, until I remembered that that was the pack and she was supposed to be in it.

I didn't want her to go, but I knew she had to. I knew I couldn't keep her, not any more. And maybe the Pattersons would catch some of the dogs but they couldn't catch all of them. I just had to hope that one of the ones that got away would be mine.

I crouched down and put my arms round her and I put my mouth right up to her ear. "You have to go," I said. And I took off her cardi and tutu.

As I did it, Dog rubbed her face against mine, and it made a sob come out of my mouth.

"I know," I said. "I don't want you to go either. But it's time."

And Dog lifted her head at that, like she was

listening to the barks of the other dogs as they got further and further into their freedom.

And then I let go.

And then she ran, after the other dogs, off out of the farm, and into freedom.

I watched her catch up with the pack, then I tried to keep my eye on her but the dogs started to blur and in the end they were just dots in the distance and I couldn't tell which was her dot, or even if she was there at all any more.

"Goodbye, Dog," I whispered.

Then I stood up, and I began the long trudge back down the lane towards home.

Every step was slow and hard and heavy, like I was wading through glue. Because each step was a step without Dog at my side to lift my heart. And each step was a step closer to Dad.

I tried to think of how I could make it up to him. Like if I did the washing-up for ten years, or never once left my pants on the floor until

I was ancient, like thirty, or if I saved all my birthday and Christmas money until I was as old as Other Nan. Only then I realised that by then Dad might not even be here any more. And it might not be enough either. I thought maybe I should've run away too. Gone to Macklin's Woods and lived off water from the stream and rabbits, like a caveman would. Only I don't know how to catch a rabbit and I don't think I'd want to eat one anyway.

So then I was thinking maybe I could be just a gatherer and eat nuts and berries, and wondering if I should turn round, when I saw the first one. I saw a dog having a wee on Mr Fazakerley's fence. Not our dog, but a greyhound all the same. Then I saw another one. This one was sitting at the bus stop, like it was waiting for the number 49. Then I heard a car honk and looked up and three more were in the road all trying to stick their noses in an old burger wrapper. The car honked again and the dogs scattered, but the car carried on honking, and flashing its lights, and that's when I saw what it was – a black Ford Fiesta Zetec.

Little Sue.

She drove past, turned the car round with a screech and pulled up next to me.

"Get in," she said.

So I did.

"Have you done what I think you've done?" she asked.

I said, "Probably."

"Where's your dog?" she asked then.

"Gone," I said. "Where's Dad?"

"At home. He was all for calling Karol to take him out in the Nissan but I said he'd be better off waiting in case you showed up."

I felt pale then, like I knew all the blood had dripped out of my head and down to my feet. "Is he all right?"

"All right?" she asked. "No he flaming isn't. He's half worried to death."

"About the Pattersons?"

Little Sue laughed then, which I thought was weird. "No," she said. "About you, you daft flapjack."

Then neither of us said anything until the car stopped outside our house.

"Good luck," said Little Sue.

"Thanks," I said.

But I knew I'd need more than luck.

I'd need a miracle.

When Dad opened the door, I thought he was going to shout, and then I thought he was going to cry, but in the end, he just stood back and let me walk into the hall, where Johnny was sitting on the staircase, and Tommo was hopping around like a flea.

"He's back!" Tommo yelled. "I knew he wouldn't escape!"

"No one's escaping," Dad said.

"He nearly did," Tommo said.

"He wasn't . . . " Dad began, then he changed his mind. "Just go to your room."

"But what about—" Tommo tried to say something but Dad cut him off.

"Room. Now. You and all, Johnny."

And I knew I was for it then. If not even they were allowed to listen.

"Follow me," Dad said.

And I did. Through the hall and into the kitchen and out the back door. Then down the path towards the shed.

I felt even sicker at that, like he was going to take me there and let me have it. Or lock me in even, and leave me there for days.

He opened the door, and I closed my eyes waiting for him to push me inside.

And I waited.

And I waited.

And I waited.

Then I felt it, a snuffle on my wrist, and then a rough tongue all over my fingers.

I made a noise, and opened my eyes.

Do you know who it was, God?

It was Dog.

We sat down in the shed then, me and Dad and Dog. All of us with our legs crossed.

"Why'd you do it, Billy?" he asked.

"To make your heart melt," I said.

Dad shook his head. "Do you think my heart's . . . frozen?" he asked.

I shook my head then. "No," I said. "Just cold and . . . a bit cross. And maybe sad from missing Mum. And tired. From all the work."

"Oh, Billy."

"I'm sorry, Dad," I said. "I didn't mean to do a bad thing."

"I know, Billy."

I looked at Dog, who was in her nest, with her toes just touching mine.

"Will she have to go?" I asked. "Back to the Pattersons, I mean."

Dad shook his head.

My heart lifted then, like it had strings pulling it up and Dad was in charge of them. "Really?" I asked.

"Really," he repeated. "Johnny told me what was going on up there. God knows why you didn't tell me before."

"You had a lot to worry about," I said. "And we thought we'd start small."

Dad made a noise then, a half laugh and half choke. "Well he won't be going back," he said.

"She," I said.

"What?"

"It's not he, it's she."

"Right," said Dad. "And does *she* have a name?"

"Dog," I said. "She's called Dog."

And I put my arms around her and hugged her as hard as I could.

And then I felt arms around me too. Dad's arms, right round me and Dog. And he was saying something in my ear, and it was, "You're incredible, do you know that?" he said. "You are The Incredible Billy Wild."

And right then I felt so full of brilliance, all bright and hot and shining, that I didn't care if we won Brimley's Got Talent, because it felt like I had anyway, and an Olympic medal and all.

Dad let go after about a minute, and wiped his eyes. "So will she sing anything?" he asked.

"Pretty much," I replied.

And Dad sang then. He did "You'll Never Walk Alone" which is his football song, and after about ten words Dog joined in. And then he laughed so hard he had to stop, and Dog stopped too. Then he did "It's Raining Men" which Tommo likes because of imagining what it would be like if men did fall out of the sky. And Dog sang again and Dad laughed even more. And every song – except for "Billie Jean" by Michael Jackson, which for some reason Dog does not like – Dog joined in and Dad laughed.

I started laughing and all then, only then the

laughing turned into something else and I realised I was crying. And I cried and cried all the tears that I'd had to stopper up all the time we'd been hiding Dog, and all the time since Mum died, then Dad hugged me again, so tight that even more squeezed out.

"Don't cry, Billy Boy," he said. "It's going to be all right. I promise."

And you know what? I believe him.

10 p.m.

The police rounded the dogs up and took them to the rescue centre. Some of them got as far as ten miles away, but most of them just stayed in the village and pooed on gardens, including Mr Hegarty's, and tried to get things out of Mrs Beasley's shop. One even got into Paris's house and sat itself on the sofa so that when her mum came back down from the loo it was watching a quiz show on telly, happy as you like. Paris sent me a photo.

Dad's still laughing. He says he'll stop in a bit, and then he'll think up a way to punish me and Tommo and Johnny for what we did. But the thing is, it doesn't really matter because whatever it is it couldn't be worse than losing Dog and he says that's never going to happen now.

He went round to the Pattersons – him and Karol and Nog – and he told them what with all the trouble they're in for keeping dogs in poor conditions, they'd be better off letting us have Dog, as it was one less for them to have to face up to in court and in the end Mr Patterson agreed, or rather I think he was scared of Nog, who has a lot of tattoos, and Karol, who is highly hairy for someone with a woman's name. Dad says there's procedures. Like she has to be cleared by the vet, and we have to be approved by the rescue people. But as long as we pass that, she's ours for good.

And Dad says we'll pass. The shed's still coming down, but he's going to build Dog a proper kennel and until then she can stay in the house with us.

Dad said it would be nice to have a lady around the house for a while.

Tommo said, "For the Woman's Touch."

Which is when Dog farted, which set everyone off laughing.

Anyway the thing is, God, I have to go because it's late now and I still have to walk Dog and also it's school in the morning. And normally I'd say "see you tomorrow" or something but I don't think I will. Not tomorrow and maybe not ever. And it's not just because homework's finished either.

It's just, the more I think about it, the more I think that none of the bad stuff that happened this week was a plague or a punishment, it was just Us Boys having accidents or like Dad says, being eejits. And none of the good stuff was a miracle it was just me trying to be excellent. Trying to be The Incredible Billy Wild.

And it's not like I don't need to talk to anyone any more because everything's perfect because it isn't. Johnny's still staring at Leia's boobs and smoking and Dad's still going on strike tomorrow and he still hasn't got a girlfriend (or a boyfriend, Tommo says, because he is highly keen on equality) and even though Dad says we'll never have to live with her, Other Nan is still going to boss us all around.

Oh, and we didn't win the talent show either. The Norton twins did, which Dad says is fair and Tommo says is highly annoying. I mainly felt sad for Paris because it was her distinct talent and also her dream, but she says she's not that bothered because Nog reckons he knows someone called Mad Harry who sings down the bingo on a Friday and he'll give her lessons after school if she likes, which she does.

But the thing is, I have other people to talk to now.

For instance Dad, who says he knows he's been caught up in work but that doesn't mean he doesn't have time for Us Boys and that we can tell him anything we want. So Tommo told him that he once did a wee in Dad's left trainer and Dad said that wasn't what he had in mind but well done for owning up.

And then there's Paris, who mostly talks while I listen but I don't mind because I like her voice, plus she said she'd pick me to be in her class at secondary if I picked her. I said what about Lacey and she said she'll put her second but I'm first because I don't tend to argue about eyeshadow primer as much. And I know there's still Seamus to deal with. Because however much trouble Mr and Mrs Patterson are in with the police – and Dad says it's Big Trouble – they won't put Seamus in prison. And he'll know it was me who kept Dog, and me who set all the other ones free, so I'll be the one in Big Trouble with him at school. But you know what? I'm not scared. Or not so much. Not now I've got Paris.

But best of all I have Dog.

And I know she doesn't answer, but to be

fair about it nor do you and at least I know she definitely exists.

So I just wanted to say goodbye, I suppose.

Goodbye then.

PS Though if you are real and if you do have a spare miracle lying around, Tommo says could you make Dad change his mind on the Cheetos and the chocolate milk. Thanks.

Acknowledgements

There are so many people I could name here, from my agent and editors who guided me, to the friends who cheered from the sidelines along the way, but most of all I want to thank the League Against Cruel Sports, which campaigns for better conditions for racing dogs, the numerous organisations across the UK that rescue retired greyhounds, and the good souls who take in the good-for-nowts and give them a home. You are all incredible.

Discover Joe's adventures in *Joe All Alone*

Available now

Truth or dare? Read Asha's story in

White Lies, Black Dare

Available now